The Case of the Prescient Poodle

A Thousand Islands Doggy Inn Mystery

B.R. Snow

Copyright © 2018 B.R. Snow

ISBN: 978-1-942691-44-0

Website: www.brsnow.net/

Twitter: @BernSnow

Facebook: facebook.com/bernsnow

Cover Design: Reggie Cullen

Cover Photo: James R. Miller

Other Books by B.R. Snow

The Thousand Islands Doggy Inn Mysteries

- The Case of the Abandoned Aussie
- The Case of the Brokenhearted Bulldog
- The Case of the Caged Cockers
- The Case of the Dapper Dandie Dinmont
- The Case of the Eccentric Elkhound
- The Case of the Faithful Frenchie
- The Case of the Graceful Goldens
- The Case of the Hurricane Hounds
- The Case of the Itinerant Ibizan
- The Case of the Jaded Jack Russell
- The Case of the Klutz King Charles
- The Case of the Lovable Labs
- The Case of the Mellow Maltese
- The Case of the Natty Newfie
- The Case of the Overdue Otterhound

The Whiskey Run Chronicles

- Episode 1 – The Dry Season Approaches
- Episode 2 – Friends and Enemies
- Episode 3 – Let the Games Begin
- Episode 4 – Enter the Revenuer
- Episode 5 – A Changing Landscape
- Episode 6 – Entrepreneurial Spirits
- Episode 7 – All Hands On Deck
- The Whiskey Run Chronicles – The Complete Volume 1

The Damaged Posse

- American Midnight
- Larrikin Gene
- Sneaker World
- Summerman
- The Duplicates

Other Books

- Divorce Hotel
- Either Ore

To Laurie and Stella

Chapter 1

I looked around the windowless white room as I rubbed my tender wrists. Five minutes ago, they'd been secured behind my back by a pair of way too tight handcuffs that had snagged skin and drawn blood. I held both hands up in front of my face to examine the red semicircles then glanced around the room again.

"This isn't too bad," I said.

"Compared to what?" Josie said, frowning.

"I don't know," I said with a shrug. "This is my first time in jail. But I guess it could be a lot worse. I was worried they were going to put us in one of those disgusting cells with a toilet in the middle of the room."

"Give them time," Josie said. "First comes the questioning, then comes lockup. After that, I'm sure we'll be making the transition to peeing in public."

"Well, aren't you the eternal optimist," I said, glancing under the table we were sitting next to.

"What on earth are you doing?"

"Just checking for listening devices," I said, running a hand along the bottom of the table.

Josie shook her head at me and stretched her legs out and arched her back.

"Okay, Columbo. Knock yourself out."

"Hey, in situations like this, you can't be too careful," I said, sitting back in the chair after my search came up empty.

"How long do you think this is going to last?"

"The questioning or the sentencing?" I said.

"The sentencing? Who's being the eternal optimist now?"

"It's a legitimate concern. Do you think we've committed a felony?" I said, glancing over at her.

"Poultry theft? A felony?" she said, shaking her head. "No, it can't be more than a misdemeanor, right?"

"I guess it depends on how valuable the birds are," I said.

"That would be a pretty fowl reason to go to prison," Josie deadpanned.

"Don't start," I said, making a face at her.

"Suzy, I'm sitting in the police station in a windowless room when I could be home snacking in bed and staring out at the ocean. You're lucky I don't have my hands around your throat."

"So, now this is all my fault," I said, pouting.

"Of course, it's your fault," she snapped. "It was your idea. And if you hadn't started mouthing off to that cop, we might not even be here facing the prospect of having to pee in public."

"I didn't like his attitude," I said, flashing back to my confrontation with the policeman.

"He's a cop, Suzy. Not the ice cream man."

"Don't mention food," I said, shaking my head. "I'm starving."

2

"Yeah, me too," Josie said. "I wonder how the food is in here."

"I'm gonna go with dreadful," I said. "But maybe Chef Claire will be able to smuggle some stuff in."

"For your sake, I sure hope so," Josie said, grinning. "Because I bet they serve their prisoners a lot of fish."

"Don't even joke about that," I said, cringing.

We glanced up when the door opened and gave the man a small wave.

"Detective Renfro," I said. "I'm surprised to see you here."

"Right back at you," the detective said, sitting down across from us and tossing a folder on the table. He glanced back and forth at us, shaking his head the entire time. "Let me start by reminding you that you are *guests* in Cayman and that the *privilege* can be revoked at any time."

"Well, technically, we're property owners," I said. "So, that must put us in a different category than your normal tourist, right?"

"Shut it," Josie whispered.

"Absolutely," Detective Renfro said, nodding. "You are definitely in a different category from normal."

"Funny," I said, frowning at him. "I was expecting to be questioned by the cops that arrested us. Why did they call you in?"

"I drew the short straw," he said, studying the contents of the folder.

3

"You're on fire tonight, Detective," I said, then a thought popped. "Should we read anything into the fact that you're working on the Jensen case and also questioning us?"

"You should not," he said, glancing up before sitting back in his chair to study what I assumed was the arrest report. "This is an impressive list of charges."

"You should be giving us a medal," I said.

"Let's see," Detective Renfro said, ignoring me as he read the report. "Burglary." He glanced up and smiled at us. "You can get up to fourteen years for that."

"What?" Josie said.

"Fourteen years?" I said, giving him a wide-eyed stare.

"Oh, good," he said. "Now I have your attention. Let's see. Illegal trespassing, theft, possession of stolen property. Well done, you hit the trifecta with that one."

"Possession of stolen property?" I said. "Who stole it?"

"You did," he said.

"That's not fair," I said. "You're double-dipping."

"Oh, you caught that?" he said, flashing a quick smile. "Verbal assault. What did you say to Officer Jones?"

"I don't remember," I said, staring off at the wall.

"Maybe your memory is better," the detective said, turning to my partner in crime.

"Oh, I'm not comfortable using that sort of language," Josie said.

"Fair enough," he said, nodding. "A couple of public nuisance charges, a possible drunk and disorderly."

"Drunk and disorderly?" I said, frowning. "What are you talking about? I haven't had a drink all night."

"I'm sure they threw that one in just because they couldn't believe any sober person would do what you did."

"We want a lawyer." I said.

"You *need* a lawyer," the detective said, again reading from the document. "Oh, and this one is always one of my personal favorites. Assaulting a police officer. Nice touch."

"I was handcuffed," I said. "How the heck could I have assaulted him?"

"You bit him."

"He was getting handsy," I said.

"Please stop talking, Suzy," Josie said, placing a hand on my arm.

"So, when can we get out of here?" I said.

"If you're lucky, sometime before you get through your childbearing years," the detective said, closing the folder and placing his elbows on the table.

"You're just trying to scare us," I whispered.

"How am I doing?" Detective Renfro said.

"You certainly got my attention," Josie said.

"Okay," Detective Renfro said as he glanced at his watch then removed a notebook from his shirt pocket. He flipped to a fresh page and jotted down a note. Then he glanced back and forth at us with an evil grin I so wanted to knock off his face. "Who wants to go first?"

"She does," Josie said, pointing at me. "It was all her idea."

"Thanks for throwing me under the bus," I said, glaring at her.

"Suzy, you're lucky I'm not *driving* the bus."

Chapter 2

Four days earlier

I stretched my legs out in front of me on the padded seat and draped my arms over the metal railing that ran across the bow of Captain Jack's charter boat that was drifting and gently rocking from a light breeze out of the west. I gazed out at the water where turquoise met cobalt blue and yawned as the motion of the boat, combined with the two Mimosas I'd put away over the past hour, tempted me into an early afternoon nap. I glanced at the stern where the love of my life was chatting and fishing with my friends Rooster and Rocco and my mom's boyfriend, Paulie. Max caught my eye, gave me a big smile and a wave I returned, then I looked back out at the water with a contented smile.

"Penny for your thoughts," Josie said as she refreshed my Mimosa then leaned back against the railing and wiggled her freshly painted toenails.

"I was just sitting here thinking about how good my life is and wondering why I've been so lucky," I said. "You know, if I were somehow able to see into the future, I don't think I'd want to look. I'd be afraid it could only go downhill from here."

"Wow," she said, taking a sip of her Mimosa. "That's gotta be worth a dollar."

"Yeah, I know," I said, laughing. "Deep, huh?"

"So, prescient abilities don't interest you?"

"Oh, good word," I said, grinning. "Much more erudite than psychic. No, I'm happy just waiting for things to unfold. What about you? Any interest in knowing what your future holds?"

"Since I do my best to limit my focus to the short-term horizon, my prescient abilities are actually well-honed. I know exactly what my future holds."

"Lunch and another Mimosa?"

"Nothing gets past you."

"What are we talking about?" my mother said, sliding onto the padded seat next to me.

"We were just discussing the ability to predict the future," I said, making room for her.

"Interesting," my mother said. "What did you come up with?"

"We haven't gotten past lunch," Josie said.

My mother nodded then gazed off into the distance.

"I'm seeing a June wedding followed by my first grandchild sometime the following spring."

"That's not a prediction, Mom," I said, laughing. "That's wishful thinking."

"Never underestimate the power of dreams, darling," she said, patting my hand as she continued to scan the open water. "Not to mention prayer. I must say that having the board meeting out here was a wonderful idea."

"It sure beats a stuffy conference room," Josie said, then perked up when she saw Chef Claire and Abby Vandenburgh, the CEO of Wags, our dog toy company, approach carrying appetizer trays.

Chef Claire and Abby placed the trays in front of us then sat down. Both were wearing swimsuits and floppy hats and sunglasses. I glanced around and realized we looked more like a group of beachgoers than we did the board of directors for a dog toy company that had taken off like a rocket since its official launch late last year.

"This is much better than having the meeting in Ottawa," Abby said, building a nosh plate. "It was minus eighteen when I flew out yesterday."

"Celsius or Fahrenheit?" Chef Claire said, raising an eyebrow.

"Does it matter?" Josie said.

"No, not really," Chef Claire said, laughing as she dipped an eggroll into a garlic plum sauce.

"Are we ready to get started?" Abby said, reaching into her bag and passing out copies of a thick, bound document.

"I believe we are," I said. "The monthly meeting of the Wags' board of directors is now in session. And I'd like to perform my first and last official duty of the day by turning the meeting over to our magnificent, and rapidly turning pink, CEO."

"Good job," Josie said, raising her Mimosa in a toast. "To the Chairwoman."

"To the Chairwoman," the others said as they completed the toast.

"We probably should have started earlier," Abby said as she poked her shoulder with a finger to test for signs of sunburn. "How many of those have you had?"

"Just enough to make it through the meeting," I said, taking a sip.

"But you better hurry," Josie said, refreshing our drinks.

"Good idea," Abby said. "I only have three things I need to go over with you, so this shouldn't take too long. Let's go through the financials first."

"Yuk," I said, frowning.

"She's such an inspirational leader," Josie said, glancing over at Chef Claire.

"Shut it."

"On page three, you'll see the summary financial statement," Abby said. "I think you'll like what you see."

"We've hit our annual revenue target already?" my mother said, glancing up from her document.

"We have," Abby said, beaming. "And if our projections are right, we're going to more than triple them by the end of the year."

"Wow," Chef Claire said. "We've definitely got a hit on our hands."

"We can't keep up with the demand," Abby said. "That's why I'm recommending we expand our manufacturing capacity as soon as possible. There's a proposal for that starting on page seven."

"A million-six," I said, studying the page. "What have we got left on our initial credit line?"

"A little over two," Abby said. "I thought we'd use a million of that and fund the rest out of our cash reserves."

I glanced around and was met with silence. I waited for several seconds, then shook my head.

"I think this is the part where you guys are supposed to ask questions."

"Is *what's for lunch* an appropriate question?" Josie said, glancing over at Chef Claire.

"Probably not," she said. "But the guest of honor is a shrimp and lobster salad on a fresh baguette."

"Is that the one with the dill remoulade?" Josie said.

"That's the one," Chef Claire said.

"Are you done?" I said, frowning at Josie.

"Yes, all my questions have been answered," she said.

"Sorry," I said to Abby with a shrug. "They probably didn't prepare you for a board of directors like this one at Wharton."

"Hey, I thought it was a great question," Abby said. "And an even better answer. It sounds fantastic."

"I think it's going to be a good one," Chef Claire said, yawning.

"Okay, I suggest you take a few days to review the expansion plan and let me know your thoughts before I fly back home. And the only other thing on the agenda is to give you an update on the tests we've been running with Chef Claire's granola and jerky."

"And?" Chef Claire said.

"Off the charts," Abby said. "The dogs go nuts over them. In fact, I included some space to produce them in the expansion plan. Victor wants to get them into his stores as soon as possible."

Victor Rollins was the CEO of Middleton Enterprises, the largest pet store franchise in North America that was the exclusive retail distributor of Wags' product line.

"He wants to discuss it with us while he's down here," Abby said.

"When does he get in?" I said.

"Today. In fact, he should have landed by now," Abby said, then smiled as she looked off into the distance.

I caught the look in her eyes and glanced over at Josie and Chef Claire who were also studying Abby's expression. Josie took a sip of her Mimosa then leaned forward.

"Is there something you'd like to tell us, Abby?" Josie said.

"What do you mean?" Abby said, turning coy.

"Come on, spill," Josie said, laughing. "I'd recognize that look anywhere."

"Well, I imagine you're going to figure it out as soon as he gets here," Abby said, leaning back against the bow railing. "Victor and I have started seeing each other."

"Good for you," I said. "How long have you two been dating?"

"We started right after Thanksgiving," Abby said. "And we haven't stopped since. Not that we have a lot of time together with everything going on with both companies."

"I'm happy for you, Abby," Chef Claire said, raising her glass. "I like Victor."

"Yeah, me too," Abby said, clinking glasses with all of us.

"Is that it for the meeting?" I said, glancing at the stern where the men were still fishing.

"Pretty much. I've got a list of some other small things we'll need to discuss, but they can wait," Abby said. "But I do need to get a few things scheduled with you."

"Like what?" I said, frowning.

"I've got several meetings coming up over the next few months that you should probably attend as Board President."

"Can it wait until after lunch?" I said.

"Sure," Abby said, exhaling audibly as she stuffed her copy of the document into her bag and draped it over her shoulder. "Let's eat."

Josie and Chef Claire hopped down off the bow onto the deck, and Abby followed them toward two large ice chests sitting next to the captain's chair. I frowned as I watched them depart.

"I think I hurt Abby's feelings," I said to my mother.

"Yes, I'm sure you did."

"What did I do?"

"Think about it," she said, staring out at the water.

I did. Several seconds later, I glanced over at her.

"She doesn't think I'm taking my role as board president seriously enough, right?"

"Bingo," my mother said. "You got it in one."

"What do you think?" I said, frowning.

"I think she's right," my mother said, shrugging.

"Really?"

"Yes. But it doesn't matter what I think, darling."

"Since when?" I said, grinning at her.

"Don't start."

I sat quietly fiddling with the document Abby had given us. I glanced out at the dark blue water and felt the sun beating down on me.

"I hate this stuff, Mom," I said, making eye contact with her.

"I know you do, darling. But this is what corporations do. And you can only expect more of the same as we move forward."

"I'm not sure I can live with that," I said, draining the last of my Mimosa.

"Then you have some decisions to make, don't you?" she said, sliding off the seat onto the deck. She put her hands on her hips as she looked around the open water. "It's so beautiful out here. Now, this is the way to spend time."

"Is that a hint, Mom?"

"No, just an observation," she said. "Come on. Let's have some lunch. You always think better after you've eaten."

Chapter 3

After lunch, in an effort to hopefully change our luck catching at least one fish, Captain Jack started the engine, and we started trolling. Fifteen minutes later, he pointed off the starboard side at what appeared to be several pieces of driftwood and a collection of seaweed hanging off them. It bobbed gently in the water and looked a bit like a patch of ill-tended landscape.

"I've got an idea," Captain Jack said, putting the boat in neutral and shutting down the engine. "Sometimes Dolphin Fish like to hang out near stuff like that. Let's try a few casts in that direction."

"Dolphin Fish?" Josie said.

"Mahi Mahi," Chef Claire said.

"Oh, I love Mahi Mahi," Josie said, softly clapping her hands. "Especially that Thai red curry you serve at the restaurant."

"I know you do," Chef Claire said. "Everyone who's ever been to the restaurant knows that."

"I would have thought you'd appreciate the standing ovation," Josie said.

I watched Rooster cast, then Max and Rocco followed suit. Moments later, all three of them were battling fish on the other end of their lines.

"How about that?" I said, glancing at Captain Jack. "You're a genius."

"Sometimes you get lucky," he said, bowing slightly.

"Man, that is one ugly fish," Josie said as she watched Rooster maneuver his fish onto the boat.

The fish was probably close to forty pounds and was green and yellow speckled with blue with a dorsal fin running the length of its body. From a color standpoint, the fish was gorgeous. But what made it ugly was the protruding forehead that dominated the fish's head. Between the forehead and what appeared to be a permanent frown etched on the fish's mouth, it reminded me of an old photo I'd seen of my bald and grumpy great-grandfather.

Max and Rocco also landed their fish, then all three cast again and within minutes each caught another. They tossed the fish into a holding container that was built into the deck then Max closed the hatch.

"That's six," Max said. "That's plenty, right?"

"They're running pretty hot at the moment," Captain Jack said. "You sure you don't want to keep fishing?"

"What would we do with them?" Max said.

"Good point," Rooster said. "Can't let them go to waste."

"We only need one for us," my mother said.

"Me too," Rocco said. "Teresa and the kids love Mahi."

"Captain Jack? Would you like one of them?" I said.

"Thanks," he said. "I've got a new smoker I'm dying to try out."

"Well, that's three," I said, then glanced at Chef Claire. "Why don't you take the other three to the restaurant?"

"You read my mind," Chef Claire said. "Who wants to give me a hand cleaning them?"

"I'm in," Rooster said. "You want to do it now?"

"Why not?" Chef Claire said, then looked at Captain Jack. "You've got a cleaning table below deck, right?"

"I do," Captain Jack said. "And just toss everything overboard when you're done. We'll give the sharks something to snack on. That is if you guys aren't planning on going in the water."

"Not anymore, I'm not," I said, laughing.

"My, what a nice boat," my mother said, staring out off the port side.

We all turned and watched a large yacht slowly make its way past us heading in the direction of Grand Cayman. A man and a woman were stretched out on deck chairs and barely managed a small wave as they passed. I noticed a dog pacing back and forth on the deck, apparently preoccupied with something.

"Is that a poodle?" Josie said, holding a hand up to her eyes to block the glare.

"Yeah, it is. A standard," I said, squinting as the sunlight bounced off the water. The dog was a gorgeous shade of brown, it's fur clipped short. "And it seems agitated."

"Yes, it does," Josie said. "Now, it's barking at them."

"And they don't seem very happy about it," I said.

I gave the couple a final wave as the yacht continued on its way. Then my mouth dropped open when I saw the poodle race across the deck to the stern and leap into the water. The poodle popped to the surface and began swimming straight toward our boat.

"What the heck is going on?" I said.

"Maybe it doesn't like being yelled at," Josie said, shaking her head. "It's heading right for us."

"This doesn't make any sense at all," I said, unable to take my eyes off the poodle that was churning through the water.

The dog eventually made it to Captain Jack's boat and swam to the stern. Josie and I leaned over the side and helped the poodle climb onto the platform that ran along the transom just above the surface of the water. We lifted her onto the boat and set her down on the deck. The poodle shook then scrambled to the bow and began barking as she stared at the yacht. Either the couple on the boat didn't realize their dog was gone or didn't care. The poodle put its front paws up on the railing and continued to bark non-stop.

Then the yacht exploded.

We all stared in disbelief at the giant fireball that seemed to be rising up from the sea. The yacht was engulfed in flames and continued to burn as several other smaller explosions followed. Captain Jack made a distress call on his radio, provided our location to the person on the other end of the line, then sat down in his captain's chair and ran a hand through his hair with a stunned expression. The poodle continued to stare at the burning boat. Josie approached the dog who accepted a head rub without taking her eyes off the yacht that was rapidly disintegrating. Another explosion followed, this one almost as loud as the first, and we heard the faint sound of wood and fiberglass cracking. Then the yacht split into two pieces and slowly sank below the surface of the water.

"Should we go check it out?" I said.

"I guess it couldn't hurt," Captain Jack whispered. "Not that there's going to be much left to see."

He started the engine and accelerated toward where the yacht had sunk. Small pieces of debris began landing in the water near us. I headed to the bow and sat down next to the dog who was stretched out on the padded seat with her head propped up on her front paws. I stroked the dog's head, and she stared up at me with a forlorn look that broke my heart. I reached for the name tag attached to the poodle's collar.

"Polly," I said.

"Cool name," Josie said. "Polly the poodle."

"This is so weird," I said, shaking my head.

"That's the word for it," Josie said. "The way she jumped off that boat. It's like she knew it was going to blow up."

"I know," I said, staring out at the smoking debris floating nearby. "But how is that possible?"

"She must have smelled something," Josie said. "Maybe there was a gas leak."

"Maybe."

"Or perhaps she can see into the future," Josie said, gently stroking the poodle's back.

"Really?" I said, scowling. "A psychic poodle?"

"Let's go with prescient. It sounds more erudite."

"Don't start."

"Polly the prescient poodle," Josie said, nodding. "I like it. It rolls off the tongue."

"You're babbling."

"I'm doing everything I can not to think about what I just saw," she whispered. "Those poor people."

"Yeah, I'm sure they never saw it coming," I said.

We both looked at the poodle who was still staring out at the water and focused on a cushion that was smoking and bobbing in the water.

"How the heck did she know?" I said.

"I have no idea," Josie said. "But she is one very lucky dog."

Then a small piece of what appeared to be bright red, leathery skin landed with a soft *plop* on the padded seat next to us. I picked it up and examined it.

"You know what that looks like?" Josie said, rubbing her fingers over the object.

"Rooster wattle?" I said, glancing at her, thoroughly confused.

"Yeah," Josie said. "I think that's what it is. Weird. You would think someone who owned a yacht that size could afford an alarm clock."

I stifled a laugh as I continued to glance around the immediate area then brushed my hand across my face to chase away what I assumed was a bug. Something else drifted across my cheek, and I frowned when I caught a glimpse of the object that was fluttering in the gentle breeze. It reminded me of a giant snowflake, but since it was eighty degrees and sunny, I discarded that notion immediately. I held my hand out, and one of the objects drifted onto my palm and settled. I stared down at it then held my hand out to Josie.

"A feather?" she said, frowning. Then we glanced up and saw dozens of them slowly making their way down onto Captain Jack's boat. "You think a seagull might have been taken out by the explosion?"

"No, that's not a seagull feather," I said, shaking my head. "It's dark brown. I'm going to go with rooster."

Then something caught Josie's eye, and I followed her stare.

"What the heck is that?" I said, studying a patch of a thin, white film floating on the surface of the water.

"It looks like some sort of powder," Josie said, then pointed. "There's more of them. A whole bunch."

"Drugs?" I said, glancing at her.

"Well, I doubt if it's baby powder."

"Roosters and drugs?" I said. "What the heck were they doing out here with that combination?"

"I'm gonna go with something illegal."

"Yeah. Good call."

Chapter 4

Captain Jack dropped anchor while we waited for the police boat to arrive. I stretched out in the bow and rested my head on Max's lap. Josie and my mom had their backs against the railing and were quietly chatting about illegal white powder and feathers floating in the breeze. Chef Claire and Rooster took advantage of the time by cleaning the six Mahi Mahi then laying them out in a cooler filled with ice. Then they joined us in the bow. Rooster slid onto the padded seat between Josie and my mother. He grabbed a fresh beer then draped his arms over their shoulders.

"What are we talking about?" Rooster said.

"Smuggling," Max said as he stroked my hair.

Josie handed Rooster one of the feathers then pointed at the filmy patches floating nearby.

"Okay," Rooster said, nodding. "I get the drug reference, but where does the feather come in?"

"We think it's a rooster feather," Josie said. "But don't worry. I don't think it's one of yours."

"Funny," Rooster said. "They had a rooster on the yacht?"

"I'm guessing roosters, as in plural," I said, turning my head to look up at Max. "You've worked on disasters in the Caribbean, haven't you?"

"Sure, several."

"What do you know about cockfighting?"

"I know it's popular in some circles throughout the region," Max said. "But I've never seen one before."

"It's illegal, right?" I said, sitting up.

"It is," Max said, nodding. "And so is cocaine smuggling. But from what we're seeing floating on the water that didn't seem to deter the folks on the yacht."

"Good point," I said, nodding.

We heard the sound of a boat approaching, and Captain Jack walked to the stern. He tied the police boat to his then three policemen followed him back to where we were sitting. I recognized one of the cops immediately.

"Hey, Detective Renfro," I said, grinning.

"You certainly do get around, don't you?" Detective Renfro said, shaking his head. Then he glanced around. "Hey, Rocco."

"How's it going, Detective?" Rocco said, shaking hands with him.

"It was a lot better a half hour ago," he said, then spent a few seconds putting names to faces. "Hi, Josie. It's nice to see you. Hey, Chef Claire."

I handled the rest of the introductions then the detective sat down and removed a notebook from his pocket.

"Okay, Captain Jack called in to report an explosion," Detective Renfro said. "Let's go from there."

"We were fishing a few hundred yards away when the yacht exploded," Captain Jack said.

"You're sure it was a yacht?"

"No doubt about it," Captain Jack said. "It had to be at least a hundred feet."

"Did you happen to get the name of the vessel?" the detective said, scribbling a note.

"Wanderlust," Captain Jack said. "I've never seen the boat around here before."

"And it exploded and sunk?"

"Right after it split in half," Captain Jack said.

"But not before the dog jumped off the boat right before the explosion," I said.

"That dog?" the detective said.

"Yes."

"Poodle, right?"

"She is," I said, rubbing the dog's head. "It was like she knew there was a problem with the boat."

"Because she jumped into the water before it blew up?" the detective said, frowning.

"Yeah."

"That's odd," Detective Renfro said, scribbling another note. "Probably smelled a gas leak."

"Maybe," I whispered.

"What is it?" the detective said, frowning at me.

"Take a look at this," I said, handing him one of the feathers.

"It's very nice," he said, examining it. Then he raised an eyebrow at me. "Leaky pillow?"

"Good one, Detective," I said. "We think it came from a rooster."

"Okay," Detective Renfro said with a blank stare that eventually turned into a small smile. "So, the rooster wasn't as smart as the dog and didn't make it off the boat in time."

"Take a look in the water," I said.

Detective Renfro and his two colleagues glanced over the edge of the boat. They studied one of the filmy patches then glanced back and forth at each other.

"Walt, you and Tom go check that out," Detective Renfro said.

The other two cops climbed back onto the police boat and slowly made their way out to one of the patches. We watched as they skimmed a sample from the surface, then glanced up at Detective Renfro and nodded.

"Coke?" Detective Renfro called out.

"Yeah, that would be my guess," the cop named Walt said.

"Okay, bag up as many samples from the other spots as you can," Detective Renfro said. "But keep them separate."

The cops nodded and went about their work. Detective Renfro scanned the water then sat back down.

"That's a lot of coke," he said. "What's the significance of the feather?"

"I think they must have also been smuggling roosters," I said.

"Cockfighting?" Detective Renfro said.

"That's the only thing I can think of," I said. "Is there cockfighting going on around here?"

"I'm sure there is," the detective said, breaking eye contact briefly. "It's quite popular in some places in the Caribbean."

"Is there any money in it?" I said.

"Sure," Detective Renfro said. "If you bet on the right bird."

"It's barbaric," Josie said.

"It is," the detective said, nodding. "But not high on anyone's radar."

"Because it only involves defenseless birds?" Josie said.

"Yeah, pretty much," Detective Renfro said.

"You sound very cavalier about it, Detective," Josie said.

"I'm sorry to disappoint you," he said, sliding his notebook back into his pocket. "But in the past month, I've dealt with three missing tourists who eventually turned up dead, a local man who got drunk and hacked up his family, several armed robberies, not to mention doing everything I could to bust up a child slavery ring that was trying to expand into the area. And now it appears that I might be dealing with another drug smuggling operation. A couple of dead roosters, although a classic case of animal cruelty, is way down my list."

The detective reached out to pet the poodle.

"Cool dog," he said. "What do you think I should do with her?"

"We'll take her," I said. "At least until you get a chance to see if anyone comes forward to claim her."

"That works," he said, getting to his feet. "Okay, I guess that's all for now. I assume you'll be down here for the next few months."

"We will," I said, then remembered something. "Say, Detective, whatever happened with the woman you were dating?"

"We're finally officially engaged," he said, beaming. "I'm very excited."

"Congratulations," I said. "When's the wedding?"

"We're still working on a date. Probably sometime in the summer," he said. "How about you?"

"What about me?" I said, frowning.

"Are there any wedding plans in your future?" he said, glancing back and forth at Max and me with a grin.

"Also, probably sometime in the summer," my mother said.

"Knock it off, Mom."

"Prescient," Josie said with a grin.

"Wishful thinking."

Chapter 5

We took the poodle back to our place on Seven Mile Beach and introduced her to our four bruisers. Al and Dente, Chef Claire's Goldens, immediately welcomed Polly with licks and their tails wagging in synchronized double-time. Captain and Chloe were more cautious with the suspected interloper at first, but after five minutes, all five dogs were racing around the lawn then paddling furiously in the pool battling for the tennis balls we tossed in. Deciding that the poodle had passed her initial exam with flying colors, we left the dogs to their own devices and headed inside to shower and change for dinner at my mom's house about a quarter mile away.

A half-hour later with sandals in hand, we strolled along the beach with all five dogs in tow. They chased tennis balls and each other back and forth to the water's edge, and we semi-successfully dodged the torrents of water they were shaking off after each trip into the shallow water near shore. A magnificent sunset dominated by orange and yellow was in progress, and by the time we reached my mom's place, the dogs were finally worn out, panting, and more than ready for a cold drink and a nap. Josie herded all five into the garage then joined Chef Claire and me near the grill where we were keeping a close eye on what Henry was preparing. He was an elderly gentleman who lived in my mother's guesthouse during the winter and in the main house the rest of the year when she was back in Clay Bay. Multi-skilled and utterly charming, Henry maintained the property and did a wide variety of tasks on my mother's behalf including handling the majority of grilling we did on a regular basis.

"That Mahi looks beautiful, Henry," Chef Claire said as she cast a loving eye at the whole fish cooking over the hot coals. "What did you hit it with?"

"I went with that lemon and garlic butter sauce you taught me," he said, reaching for a large spatula and a set of tongs.

"Oh, good call," Chef Claire said, nodding.

"You want to give me a hand flipping him?" Henry said, handing her the tongs. "I'd hate to have him break on us."

I watched them expertly turn the fish over then focused on the chicken breasts that were cooking on the other side of the grill.

"So, the Wanderlust blew up before your eyes today," Henry said, wiping his hands with a towel. "I'm sorry you had to see something like that."

"You're familiar with the yacht?" I said, frowning.

"Yes, I've seen it around from time to time," Henry said. "But I didn't know the Jensens."

"Did they live down here?" I said.

"No, but I think one of their kids does," he said, taking a sip of beer.

"Do you know what they did for a living?" I said.

"You mean apart from smuggling dope?" he said, raising an eyebrow.

"You knew they were involved in that?" I said.

"No, your mom told me what happened," Henry said. "I had no idea. I'd heard they had some sort of import-export business."

"Interesting," I said. "Do you know what sort of stuff they dealt with?"

"You mean, apart from coke, right?" Josie deadpanned.

"Yeah, apart from that," I said, making a face at her.

"I wouldn't have a clue," Henry said, nodding at the man my mother was chatting with near the pool. "But I know who would."

I glanced at the pool then back at Henry.

"Of course," I said, grinning. "You're so good."

"Try not to annoy him before dinner," Henry said, turning back to the grill.

Josie and Chef Claire's laughter followed me as I headed to a table near the pool where my mother and Paulie were sitting with Gerald, her good friend who was also the Finance Minister of the Cayman government. All three looked up at me, and Gerald pulled the empty chair next to him back to give me room to sit down.

"Good evening," I said. "How are you, Gerald?"

"I've had better days," he said. "I'm so sorry you had to witness that this afternoon."

"Thanks," I said with a small shrug. "I just feel bad for the folks on the boat." I paused then cocked my head at Gerald. "The Jensens, right?"

"Please don't start, darling," my mother said, slowly stirring her drink as she stared at me.

"Start what, Mom?" I said as I reached over to pet Queen, her King Charles spaniel that, as usual, was parked on her lap. "I just heard their name mentioned, that's all."

"Yes," Gerald said, nodding. "Jack and Jill Jensen."

"Jack and Jill?" I said, frowning. "As in, went up the hill?"

"That's the one," Gerald said. "And we think there were at least three crew members onboard as well. Tragic."

"It certainly was," I said. "I heard they were in the import-export business."

"Darling, please."

"It certainly doesn't take you long, does it?" Gerald said with a small laugh.

"I'm just trying to get some information so we can figure out what to do with their dog," I said, deflecting.

"Of course, you are," my mother said, shaking her head. "Give it a rest, darling. It's been a very tough day for some folks around here."

"Yeah, I imagine all the coke dealers are in mourning," I whispered.

Gerald cringed then took a long sip of his drink. He exhaled loudly and stared at me.

"Okay, let's get this over with," he said, sitting back in his chair and draping a leg over his knee.

"You don't have to humor her, Gerald," my mother said.

"No, it's all right," Gerald said. "And she's not going to stop until she gets all her questions answered."

"You know me so well," I said, grinning at him.

"They have a daughter who lives down here," Gerald said. "She would be the person to talk to about the dog." Then he frowned at me. "Did the dog really jump off the boat just before it blew up?"

"She did," I said. "And it was like the dog knew something bad was about to happen."

"Probably smelled the gas leak," Gerald said.

"So, that's the official story?" I said. "The boat had a gas leak?"

"Official story?" Gerald said. "What are you insinuating, Suzy?"

"I'm not insinuating anything," I said. "It just seems odd that a high-end yacht like that would blow up from something as mundane as a gas leak. Especially if they had a full-time crew working on it. You would think someone would have seen or smelled something."

"Accidents happen," Gerald said.

"It does seem odd," Paulie said.

"Thank you," I said, flashing him a smile.

"Don't encourage her, Paulie," my mother said, shaking her head.

"I'm just saying," he said, shrugging. "And I think I smelled diesel fumes."

"So?" Gerald said.

"Diesel will explode eventually, but it's not nearly as flammable as gasoline," Paulie said. "It just seems strange that a diesel-powered yacht would explode the way it did. I would have expected to see a big fire, but not an explosion like that."

"Unless the fuel had been leaking for a long time," Gerald said. "Maybe there were hundreds of gallons sitting in the bilge and something electrical sparked."

"It's possible," Paulie said with an indifferent shrug. "But it sounded like a bomb went off."

"Most explosions do," Gerald said, agitated.

"New topic, please," my mother said.

"Do you know the Jensen's daughter?" I said.

"I do," Gerald said. "Her name is Jennifer."

"The family sure had a thing for the letter J," I said. "Jennifer Jensen. She's single?"

"She is," Gerald said. "And I'm sure she's currently in mourning, so please tread carefully with her."

"Of course," I said, my mind racing. "You're probably not going to like my next question."

"Thanks for the warning," Gerald said, focusing on me.

"Did you know the Jensens were involved in drug smuggling?"

Gerald cringed again and took a few moments to calm himself down.

"I did not," Gerald said, shaking his head. "But it certainly does help to explain a few things."

"Like what?" I said, frowning.

"Like, none of your business," he said, laughing.

"A little snarky there, Gerald," I said, laughing along. "What sort of things did their company sell?"

"It was a lot of Asian products," he said. "Fabrics and clothing, spices and food items, and I think they did some stuff with antiques."

"So, they spent a lot of time in Asia?" I said.

"I'm sure they did," Gerald said, reaching for his drink.

"Is that where they developed their interest in cockfighting?"

Gerald gave me a wide-eyed stare.

"What on earth are you talking about?"

"Cockfighting," I said. "You know, big roosters, probably pumped full of steroids, with metal blades attached to their feet trying to kill each other."

"I know what it is, Suzy," Gerald said. "But what makes you think the Jensens were involved with it?"

"Probably because of all the rooster combs and wattles that fell from the sky right after the explosion. Along with the feathers."

Gerald squinted at me with a deep frown etched on his face.

"Really?" he said after a long pause.

"Yeah," Paulie said. "I got hit by one of the beaks."

"Do you know if they were going to be visiting their daughter?" I said.

"I'm sure they were," Gerald said. "It's about the only reason they ever visited. At least, I thought it was."

"Darling, if you upset their daughter by asking her a bunch of invasive questions, I'll never forgive you."

"You always have before, Mom," I said, going for a joke that fell flat. I waited out the glare she was giving me then focused on Gerald. "Is there cockfighting going on around here?"

"I'm sure there is," he said, shrugging.

"But you don't do anything to stop it?" I said, my voice rising.

"Suzy, I'm the Finance Minister, not the Police Commissioner," Gerald said.

"Yeah, I get that. But still. There must be something you could do. It's barbaric."

"It is," he said, nodding. "But it's way down my list of things to worry about. I'm sorry."

"Who would I talk to?"

"You're not going to talk to anyone about it," my mother said. "It's none of your business."

"Sure, sure."

"Lord, give me strength," my mother said, shaking her head. "Or at least another cocktail."

"Henry's waving at us," Paulie said, standing up. "Let's go eat."

I followed them to a long table that was set in the middle of the lawn and sat down next to Max and gave him a hug and a kiss. Josie and Chef Claire sat down across the table from us.

"Where have you been?" he said, gently squeezing my hand.

"I was just tormenting my mom and Gerald," I said, glancing around at the array of dishes on display.

"Again?" Max said, laughing.

"Still," I said, reaching for a bowl of fruit salad. "I was trying to figure out how to get in touch with someone about the poodle."

"And?"

"And then we transitioned into cockfighting," I said, munching on a piece of mango. "The conversation sort of went downhill from there."

"I guess some people just don't get your whimsical side," Max said, passing me a tray of chicken.

"Aren't you sweet," I said, giving him a kiss on the cheek.

"Whimsy? Yeah, that's the problem," Josie said, laughing.

38

"I don't remember asking you for your opinion," I said, frowning at her.

"Hey, if I waited to be asked, I'd never get a word in."

Chapter 6

After dinner, I left Max sitting with the other men as soon as they lit Cuban cigars and a cloud of smoke formed then hovered over the dinner table. I nodded at Josie and Chef Claire, and they followed me across the lawn to a small table near the pool. We sat down, and they both stared at me.

"What's on your mind?" Josie said. "You've been acting strange all night."

"Yeah, and it's really hard to tell what that happens," Chef Claire said, laughing. "So, something is definitely up."

"I don't know how to say it," I said, staring off into the night sky.

"Has something happened between you and Max?" Josie said.

"No, things are great."

"Are you sick?" Chef Claire said.

"No."

"Then how bad can it be?" Josie said, then sat back in her chair when she saw my mother approaching.

"What are you three up to huddled way over here in the corner?" my mother said, glancing around the table.

"Suzy was just about to tell us that," Josie said. "Have a seat."

"Yeah, that's a good idea," I said, pulling a chair back for her. "This concerns you as well."

"Oh, I don't think I like the sound of this," my mother said, sitting down and patting my hand.

"I feel terrible about doing this," I said.

"Just go ahead and spit it out," Josie said. "We'll figure out a way to deal with whatever it is."

"It's Wags," I said.

"Wags?" Josie said. "Okay, what about it?"

"I hate it," I blurted.

"You hate dog toys?" Chef Claire said.

"No, I hate owning a company that makes dog toys," I said. "And I especially hate being the president of the board."

"I see," Josie said with a grin.

"I love the company and what it does," I said. "It's just not for me. And I'm afraid it's going to start taking up way too much of my time. I've spent my whole life avoiding everything corporate, and all of a sudden, I'm stuck right in the middle of corporate central. I want to spend my time working on the stuff I love doing."

"Like eating and taking care of dogs," Chef Claire said.

"And planning our new rescue program," Josie said.

"Exactly," I said, nodding. "That's what I want to spend my time doing. Along with running the Inn and the rescue program down here. And we've also got the restaurants. I'm so sorry. I feel terrible about letting you guys down, but I'm already miserable, and all the crap I really hate has barely started."

Josie and Chef Claire smiled at each other then looked at my mother.

"You want to tell her?" Josie said to Chef Claire.

"No, you go ahead," Chef Claire said. "You say it much better than I do."

"Tell me what?" I said, glancing around the table.

"We want out, too," Josie said. "And we've been trying to figure out a way to tell you for about a month."

"You want out?" I said, stunned. "Why?"

"For the same reason you do," Chef Claire said. "I'm a chef, not some corporate board person. At first, it was a cool idea and a lot of fun getting it off the ground. But now, it's all going to be about quarterly growth, marketing campaigns, and meetings. Don't even get me started on the meetings. And who knows what other crap we'll have to deal with."

"What she said," Josie said, nodding at Chef Claire.

"I think it's a wonderful idea," my mother said. "I've been hoping you'd eventually come to your senses. You have much more important things to worry about, darling." Then she whispered under her breath. "Like giving me at least one grandkid."

"Wow," I said, rubbing my forehead. "This is certainly going a lot better than I expected."

42

"You do tend to tie yourself into knots worrying about nothing," Josie said. "I'm so relieved."

"So, what do we do?" I said. "We've got a small fortune sunk into the thing. Not to mention the livelihoods of all the people who work for us."

"We sell it," my mother said, shrugging.

"But it's such a new company. Who'd want to buy it?"

"Who do you think?" my mother said, nodding at the dinner table where Abby was snuggling with Victor Rollins, the CEO of Middleton Enterprises.

"You think Victor would be interested?" I said.

"Victor would probably be willing to give you one of his arms to buy Wags," my mother said. "A successful startup he's already got the exclusive distribution rights to? Think about it, darling."

"That's exactly why I want out, Mom. So I don't have to think about things like that."

"Point taken," she said, nodding. "But I'd be shocked if Victor wasn't interested in buying it."

"What about Abby?" I said.

"What about her?"

"We need to make sure she's taken care of," I said. "I feel like we're pulling the rug out from underneath her."

"From what I've seen tonight, I don't think Victor is going to let Abby get very far away," my mother said. "And she's obviously doing a wonderful job as CEO. He'd be crazy to remove her."

"But it's such a big change," I said.

"Trust me, darling," my mother said. "If there's one thing Abby is good at, it's dealing with change. And it's not like we'd be moving to another planet. I'm sure we'll figure out a way to stay in touch with her."

"I wonder what the company is worth," Josie said.

"I wouldn't have a clue," Chef Claire said, then shrugged. "And that's probably another good reason for us not to be involved in it."

"Excellent point," Josie said.

"I have no idea what it's worth," I said, frowning.

"It's in the neighborhood of fifteen million," my mother said. Then she caught the look we were giving her. "It's really not that hard to calculate."

"You've been talking to Gerald, haven't you?" I said, raising an eyebrow.

"Maybe a bit," she said, deflecting. "After your comment on the boat this afternoon, I had a chat with him and showed him the document Abby shared with us on the boat."

"You knew I wanted out," I said.

"It really wasn't that hard to figure out, darling. I was just waiting for you to find the courage to bring it up."

"Fifteen million?" Chef Claire said.

"Yes," my mother said. "And Gerald suggested that we also ask for some Middleton stock to sweeten the deal. He's so smart."

"We're each going to make three million?" Chef Claire said, stunned.

"And undoubtedly leave several million more on the table," my mother said. "That is something to consider. But that's where having the Middleton stock comes in. You know, to soften the blow of walking away from all those future earnings."

"Is this going to be a problem for you, Mom?"

"Absolutely not," she said, waving it away. "At my age, I don't need the hassle. As far as I'm concerned, it's a rounding error."

"A rounding error," Josie said, laughing. "You're my hero, Mrs. C."

"Thank you, dear. That's very sweet," my mother said, beaming at her. "Are you sure you two will be okay with that sort of deal?"

"Three million?" Josie said. "Yeah, I think I'll be able to manage."

"It's three million more than I thought I'd ever have," Chef Claire said. "But it sort of feels like I'm stealing it."

"Nonsense," my mother said. "You saw an amazing business opportunity, put a plan together, then executed it. You've earned every nickel."

"That's right," Josie said, laughing. "We were prescient."

"Not to mention incredibly lucky," I said.

"Well, there is some luck involved I must admit," my mother said. "But like they say, luck is merely a matter of preparation meeting opportunity."

"They say that, do they?" I said, laughing.

"I'm sure they do," my mother said, glancing at Max who was approaching our table with a very sad look on his face. "What on earth is the matter, Max?"

Max sat down and placed a hand on mine.

"I just got a phone call," he said.

"Oh, no," I said. "What happened?"

"A seven-point earthquake just hit Mexico," he whispered. "I need to fly out first thing in the morning."

"I can't believe it," I said, shaking my head. "Man, we can't catch a break, can we?"

"It does seem like there's a force out there that's trying to keep us apart," Max said.

"But we're not going to let that happen, are we?" I said, brushing his face gently with the back of my hand.

"We most certainly aren't," he said. "And I would like to take this opportunity to show you how committed I am to that idea."

"We should probably wait awhile," I said, flushing with embarrassment. "At least until the party thins out a bit."

Max laughed and grabbed my hand and gently pulled me to my feet.

"No, you idiot. I'm not talking about that. Follow me."

Max led me to the edge of the pool and positioned me in the moonlight. I glanced around, thoroughly confused. Then he removed a small box from his pocket and dropped to one knee.

"I know I'm probably doing this way too early, but as soon as I figured out who I wanted to spend the rest of my life with, I decided there was no reason to wait. I can't imagine my life without you at the center, and I think it's time we got started doing just that. Suzy, will you marry me?"

I flinched, then stared at him as tears streamed down my cheeks. I looked at my mom who was bawling, then at Josie and Chef Claire who were also tearing up. I managed a small nod, then took a step back to give Max room to slide the ring on my finger. My sandal caught the edge of one of the pool tiles, and my knees wobbled. I windmilled my arms in an attempt to recover my balance, teetered on the edge, then toppled backward into the pool. I surfaced, choked and spit water, then used both hands to brush the hair back from my face.

"Smooth," Josie said, shaking her head.

"Shut it. Oh, crap. I dropped the ring."

"Well, this is going well," my mother said, staring down at me. "That was a yes, right?"

"Oh, yeah," I said, beaming at Max. "It's a total yes."

"Thank ya, Jesus," my mother said looking up at the heavens.

"Okay," Josie said to Chef Claire. "You help Esther Williams out of the pool so she can give her fiancé a big kiss. I'll see if I can find the ring."

I climbed out of the pool with Chef Claire's assistance then Josie dove into the pool, searched the bottom, and surfaced moments later holding the ring. Max gently slid it onto my finger, and I stared down, dripping water, and beamed as it glistened in the moonlight.

"It fits perfectly," Max said, holding my hand up to the light.

"It certainly does."

And it felt fantastic.

Chapter 7

I pulled into a parking spot in front of the terminal and turned the jeep off. I immediately leaned over into the passenger seat to give Max a kiss and a long hug he returned before hopping out of the vehicle.

"I wish you weren't leaving," I said, watching as he slung a garment bag over his shoulder.

"Me too," he said, walking around to the driver's side to give me another kiss. "Hopefully, I won't be gone too long."

"What are you going to be doing down there?"

"They want me to help coordinate the initial relief efforts," Max said, glancing at his watch. "There's going be at least a dozen organizations helping out, and we want to make sure everyone's pulling in the same direction."

"Any idea how long you'll be gone?" I said, fiddling with my engagement ring.

"I'll have a better idea once I get on the ground," he said, again glancing at his watch. "I'll give you a call as soon as I can."

"Go," I said, nodding at the terminal. "You're running late."

He gave me a final hug and kiss then started off with a wave. He stopped and called out.

"And if you get a chance, start thinking about wedding dates," he said, then took a few steps before stopping again and looking back at me. "Or we could just sub-contract everything out to your mom."

I laughed and continued to stare after him until he disappeared from sight. I started the jeep, then grabbed the directions to Jennifer Jensen's place Gerald had written down for me last night. Ten minutes later, I turned into a residential neighborhood and located the comfortable single-story home tucked away on a cul de sac. I parked in front of the house and was about to ring the doorbell when I heard the sound of voices and splashing water coming from the back of the property. I followed a stone path around the outside of the house to a kidney-shaped pool that dominated the backyard.

A man and a woman were sprawled out on a two-seater lounge chair, and I headed in their direction. They were still wet from their recent swim and had towels draped over their shoulders. Both were drinking Caybrew, a local beer I enjoyed, especially in the late afternoon on really hot days. But since it was just after nine in the morning, I'd be politely demurring should I be offered one.

The man spotted me, exhaled a cloud of smoke, and I picked up the unmistakable scent of weed. They both grinned up at me, and the man offered me the freshly-lit joint that was the size of an egg roll.

"Hey," he said. "Want a hit?"

"No, thanks," I said, smiling as I shook my head. "It only makes me hungry."

"What's wrong with that?" he said, still holding the joint in the air.

"I have a strict policy against using performance-enhancing drugs," I said with a small shrug.

"Okay," he said, confused. "How about a beer?"

"Thanks, but no. I never drink before noon."

"You got a lot of rules, don't you?"

"Not really. Just a strong will," I said, smiling at the couple.

"Yeah, me too," he said. "But I've got a really weak won't."

He and the woman cackled. He handed her the joint, she took a long, slow drag on it, and I waited several seconds until she exhaled and her eyes were able to focus on me.

"Are you here for the party?" she said.

"No," I said, glancing at three people who were lounging in the shallow end of the pool. "Actually, I'm looking for Jennifer Jensen."

"I think she's in the house," the woman said. "Just head on in. We're pretty informal around here."

"Thanks," I said. "Have fun."

"Oh, we will," the woman said, laughing.

"Yeah, and if you change your mind about partying, just stop back. We'll be here. It's gonna be a non-stop, all-day rage."

"*Excellent*. It's good to have goals," I said, giving them two thumbs up as I wheeled around and headed across the patio toward the back door.

I knocked on a set of sliding glass doors and waited. Then I knocked again and eventually slid one of the doors open and poked my head inside.

"Hello?" I called out.

Then I heard the sound of bare feet padding across tile, and a woman came into view. She was probably in her late twenties with close-cropped pink hair that caught me by surprise when I first saw it. She frowned when she saw me and came to a stop a few feet away.

"Hi. Can I help you?" she said, folding her arms across her chest.

"Hi, I'm Suzy Chandler. Are you Jennifer Jensen?"

"I am."

"It's nice to meet you. I'd like to start by offering my condolences about your parents."

She stared at me, dry-eyed, then nodded.

"Thank you," she whispered. Then she glanced down at my hand. "That's a beautiful ring."

"Thanks," I said, grinning down at it. "I just got engaged last night."

"Congratulations," she said, then stared hard at me. "Have we met before?"

"No, I'm actually here about your folks' dog," I said. "Polly."

"She's dead, right?"

"No, she's not. I have her."

"What?" she said, confused. "How is that possible?"

"We were fishing in the vicinity of the explosion yesterday. And right before the boat…blew up, Polly jumped into the water and swam toward us. She's safe and sound."

Jennifer Jensen sat down and shook her head.

"That dog," she whispered. "I can't believe it. But I guess I shouldn't be surprised."

"I'm sorry," I said, sitting down across from her. "I'm not following you."

"There's something very weird about that dog," she said, finally managing to make eye contact.

"She's really smart," I said.

"She's spooky smart," she said. "But that's not what I'm talking about. I'm positive that dog has a sixth sense. It freaks me out."

"Sixth sense?" I said, raising an eyebrow.

"It's like she's got some sort of psychic power," Jennifer said, shaking her head. "I know that must sound really strange."

"Yeah, that's the word for it," I said, laughing.

"You think I'm joking?" Jennifer said, her voice rising a notch.

"No, but it does sound like a bit of an exaggeration."

"The last time my folks were here, my dad was sitting in a chair underneath that giant palm out by the pool. And all of a sudden, Polly started growling and barking at him. She finally got my dad's attention, and we thought she just wanted him to take her for a walk. Two minutes after he got up from his chair, a giant coconut fell off the palm and landed right where he'd been sitting. I don't know if it would have killed him, but it fell about sixty feet."

"It must have been a coincidence, right?" I said, frowning.

"That's what we all thought at the time," Jennifer said. "Then three days later, one of my uncles who was visiting decided he was going to go windsurfing. Polly went nuts when she heard him say it, and she started barking and growling again. And when my uncle was loading his equipment into his truck, she went nuts and grabbed one of his ankles and wouldn't let go."

"Really?" I said, leaning forward.

"She tore up his ankle pretty good, and my uncle was furious with her," Jennifer said. "He told my dad that he should consider putting the dog down because she must have some sort of brain tumor."

"What happened?"

"We don't know," Jennifer said. "But two days later, his body washed up on shore."

"Wow," I said, stunned. "That's amazing."

"She was always doing stuff like that," Jennifer said. "Another time she stretched out in front of the gardener's truck and wouldn't budge. It turns out that he'd gotten a flat tire, had started putting the spare on but had gotten called away. Then he forgot to put the rest of the lug nuts on. If Polly hadn't done what she did, there's a good chance the tire would have come off while he was driving home." She exhaled loudly and shook her head as if trying to clear the cobwebs away. "That dog freaks me out."

"Does that mean you don't want me to bring her here?"

"I don't want that dog anywhere near me," she said.

"Okay," I said, frowning.

"The dog knew the boat was going to blow up?" Jennifer said.

"I think so," I said. "She definitely made sure she got off the boat before it did."

"Was she barking before she jumped in the water?"

"Actually, she was," I said, flashing back to what I'd witnessed yesterday.

"And they ignored her, didn't they?" she said, shaking her head.

"Yes, I believe they did."

"My folks had a hard time believing that a dog could possess that ability," Jennifer said.

"Again, I'm so sorry for your loss."

"Yeah, thanks," she said, slowly shaking her head. "I can't believe they're gone." Then she exhaled loudly and did her best to perk up. "So, you'll find a good home for Polly?"

"We will," I said, nodding. "Can I ask you a question?"

"Sure."

"It's probably going to sound a bit strange."

"Stranger than a psychic dog?" Jennifer said, cocking her head at me.

"Fair point," I said, nodding. "What do you know about cockfighting?"

She stared at me then laughed.

"You weren't joking. That is a strange question," she said. "And my answer is probably going to sound even stranger. I know far too much about cockfighting than I care to admit."

"You do?" I said, completely taken aback.

"It was a disgusting...let's be generous and call it a hobby, that my father developed a fondness for during his travels in Asia."

"Interesting."

"Not really," Jennifer said. "It's cruel. While I'm not much of an animal lover, I despise seeing any creature tortured for so-called sport."

"Why do you think your father enjoyed it?"

"Some people bet football. My father liked to bet on armed roosters. As you can imagine, it's not part of our family legacy I like to talk about." Then she frowned and stared at me. "How do you know about the cockfighting?"

"After your parents' boat exploded, several pieces of dead rooster landed on our boat," I said, grimacing. "And us."

"Yuk," Jennifer said, then shrugged. "He must have been bringing in some ringers he'd picked up during his travels." She shook her head. "Anything to get a betting edge. He was worth a fortune, but nothing made him happier than winning a couple grand at a cockfight."

"So, there are cockfights held around here?"

"I'm sure there are," Jennifer said. "Why do you ask? You interested in trying your luck with the *bladed warriors*?"

"Bladed warriors?"

"That's what my father liked to call them. He thought they were a noble breed."

"Noble, but not worth living?"

"My sentiments exactly. So, you aren't interested in betting on them?"

"Actually, I'd like to see the roosters turn their blades on the people who've trained them to fight."

"Yeah, I'd pay to see that," Jennifer said, finally relaxing a bit. "Can I get you something to drink?"

"No, I'm good. Thanks. You're having a party today?"

"No, but I'm sure my houseguests are," she said, glancing out at the pool. "It's what they do when they're down here."

"Where are they from?" I said, also glancing outside.

"All over the place," Jennifer said. "They work for my father. At least they did."

My interest piqued, I sat up straighter in my chair.

"They work for his import-export company?"

"They do," she said. "I'm not exactly sure what all of them do, but the couple on the double recliner handles all the clothing and fabric lines."

"Interesting work," I said, nodding.

"I guess," she said, shrugging. "If you call going into poor, remote areas of the world offering natives a dollar for something you're going to sell for a hundred in the States interesting."

"Can I ask you another question?"

"Is it as good as the one about cockfighting?"

"Probably not," I said, grinning. "I was just wondering about all the cocaine."

"Yes, so were the police," Jennifer said. "They said there were dozens of spots where it had collected on the surface of the water."

"There were," I said, then paused.

"Go ahead and ask," Jennifer said, calmly waiting for me to continue.

"Okay. Did you know your father was involved in drug smuggling?"

"Smuggling? Maybe it was only for his personal use," she said, turning coy.

"And maybe he was actually a bird lover."

"Touché," she said, nodding. "No, I wasn't aware he was smuggling coke. But I can't say that I'm surprised."

"Why not?"

"I'd overheard him and my mom a few times talking about their cash flow problems," Jennifer said. "Which I attributed to him going through an extended losing streak."

"So, he bet on other things besides cockfighting?"

"I once watched my father win ten thousand dollars betting on what time it was," Jennifer said.

"How the heck did he do that?"

"He cheated."

"He snuck a peek at his watch?"

"No, he had me do it," she said, shrugging. "Then I used hand signals."

"And you got away with it?" I said, frowning.

"I was nine. And like my father said, who would ever suspect a nine-year-old girl?" she said, shrugging. "We started drifting apart soon after that."

"That's so sad," I whispered. "What do you do for work?"

"Not much at the moment," she said. "But you're looking at the new owner of Jensen International. Up until yesterday, my *job* has been to live here and take care of the house. And serve as hostess when that horde of vultures out by the pool descends every few months."

"Are you planning on running the company?"

"I guess that depends on what the police decide to do with me."

"The police don't think the explosion was an accident?"

"Let's say they're less than convinced that is was."

"And they think you might have killed your parents?"

"The estranged daughter of a wealthy couple who's the sole heir to their fortune?" Jennifer said, managing a small laugh. "I'm sure you can put two and two together."

"Math's never been one of my strong points," I said. "But I get what you're saying. You were estranged from both your parents?"

"I was."

"What was your mom like?"

"Mostly, absent," Jennifer said, then glanced at the sliding doors. "Maybe you should have brought Polly with you today."

"Why's that?" I said, confused.

"Because we probably would have had some advance notice that the cops were on their way," Jennifer said, getting to her feet. "Good morning, Detective Renfro."

60

Chapter 8

After chatting briefly with Detective Renfro, who was initially surprised to see me, I said my goodbyes and headed outside. My plan to have another talk with the couple sitting around the pool was thwarted when I realized they were both taking a nap. I imagine a twelve-pack of Caybrew and a joint the size of an egg roll before nine can put a crimp in your plans for a non-stop, all-day rage.

I drove to the animal rescue center we had established on the outskirts of Georgetown and parked in front. Josie had already arrived and was chatting with Teresa, the woman who managed the facility. I gave both of them a hug, then Teresa grabbed my left hand and examined the engagement ring.

"It's gorgeous," she said, giving me another hug. "Congratulations."

"Thanks," I said, beaming at the ring.

"Did you guys set a date yet?" Teresa said.

"No, but it will probably be sometime in the summer," I said. "If my mother has anything to say about it."

"And she does," Josie said, laughing. "Did you speak with the daughter?"

"I did."

"What's she like?" Josie said.

"She's nice," I said, frowning. "But she doesn't seem to be grieving. At least, not in any way I'd recognize."

"She wasn't close to her parents?" Josie said.

"No, not at all. And Detective Renfro popped in just before I left her place," I said. "Apparently, the cops don't think the explosion was an accident."

"That makes sense," Josie said, shrugging. "We don't either. Do the cops think she might have been behind it."

"She seems to think so," I said. "But I couldn't get anything out of Detective Renfro."

"Oh, don't you just hate when that happens," Josie said, laughing.

"Yeah," I said, grinning. "He's such a by the book kind of guy."

"Don't worry, I'm sure you'll wear him down," Teresa said.

"What did the daughter have to say about the dog?" Josie said.

"She doesn't want anything to do with it," I said.

"You want to bring her over here?" Teresa said.

"No, I think we'll keep her at the house for a few days," I said. "Jennifer is convinced that the dog has some sort of psychic power. And she said it freaks her out having her around."

"Really?" Josie said.

I spent a few minutes giving them the recap of my conversation with Jennifer then both Josie and Teresa frowned.

"Well, we're used to dogs anticipating what's going on or how we're feeling," Josie said.

"Yeah, but that's just part of the normal bond dogs develop with the people they live with, right?" I said. "Knowing that a coconut is about to fall on somebody's head or jumping off a boat just before it blows up is something else altogether."

"It does seem odd," Teresa said. "So, what are you going to do with the dog?"

"Try to find her a good home, I guess," I said. "She's a great dog. It shouldn't be that hard to find someone who'll take good care of her."

"I'm sure the dog will let us know when she meets them," Josie said.

"Don't start," I said, shaking my head.

"Or maybe we can set her up with her own 900 number," Josie said. "The Psychic Dog Hotline. I wonder if she's any good at predicting football. We'd make a fortune."

"Oh, thanks for the reminder," I said, nodding. "Jennifer said her father was an inveterate gambler. And he loved betting on cockfights."

"That's disgusting," Teresa said. "I detest that activity."

"That's right, you grew up around here," I said. "You're familiar with it?"

"I am," Teresa said. "My ex-husband used to go all the time."

"Do you know where it takes place?" I said.

"No, I don't. Why do you ask?" Teresa said.

"I'm just curious," I said, deflecting.

Josie snorted.

"Shut it."

"You want to go to a cockfight?" Josie said.

"Not unless we absolutely have to," I said. "But it would be good to know where it is just in case."

"Just in case why?" Josie said, staring at me.

"Horrible sentence structure."

"Don't change the subject," Josie said. "Answer the question."

"It would be good to know where it takes place just in case we wanted to take a look at the people who are there," I said.

"You think the cockfighting is somehow connected to that yacht blowing up?" Josie said.

"Maybe," I said, letting the idea marinate. "But I'm convinced it wasn't an accident. And since there were cocaine and roosters on the boat, it's only logical to assume that we might find cocaine dealers at the cockfight. And if we did, I think we could be close to figuring out who blew the boat up." I noticed the strange look Teresa was giving me. "What?"

"I was just wondering what it's like living with your brain," Teresa said.

"Most days it's like a runaway train on a circular track," I said, shrugging.

"And on some days, it just disappears down a long, dark tunnel," Josie said.

"But it always leaves the station, right?" Teresa said, laughing.

"Sadly, yes," I said.

Chapter 9

We were sitting at the bar sipping wine while we waited for the rest of our group and intermittently chatting with Rocco, who was doing his best to keep up with the three-deep crowd at the bar and the drink orders arriving from the packed dining room. Tony, one of the other bartenders who worked at C's Cayman, came back to the bar carrying two cases of beer and quickly began restocking a cooler. When he finished, he headed off again. Rocco finally got a chance to catch his breath, and he approached and refilled our glasses.

"What the heck is going on?" I said.

"A cruise ship came in today," Rocco said, taking a long swig of water then wiping sweat from his forehead. "And the word keeps spreading about how good the food is here."

"Thanks to all the concierges on the boats, right?" Josie said.

"Hey, it never hurts to feed and water the people who have the power to refer," Rocco said, laughing. "Who are you waiting for?"

"Abby and Victor Rollins. And my mom. Chef Claire said she was going to join us if she had a few minutes, but I don't like her chances," I said. "Man, I can't believe how busy it is."

"Hold that thought," Rocco said, heading to the other end of the bar.

"I love this place," Josie said, glancing around. "I'm so glad we opened it."

"Me too," I said, waving at Abby and Victor as they came through the front door. "Hi, guys."

"Hey," Victor said, taking in the crowd. "Wow, when Abby said it was a popular place, I had no idea this was what she was talking about."

"Do you know what the special is tonight?" Abby said, giving both of us hugs.

"I think it's the Mali red curry," Josie said.

The front door opened again, and my mother entered and made her way toward us.

"A cruise ship must have landed today," she said as she shook hands with Abby and Victor then hugged us. "So much for a quiet business meeting."

My mother waved to our hostess who gestured for us to follow her to a table set for six in a back corner of the dining room. She passed out menus then slowly worked her way back through the crowd.

"I got a call from one of our largest franchises today," Victor said. "And she said she can't keep the toys in stock. Apparently, word of mouth is driving people to her store in droves."

"That's great," I said, without much enthusiasm.

"Geez, Suzy," Victor said, laughing. "Dial down the excitement."

"Yeah, sorry," I said, shrugging.

"What on earth is the matter?" Victor said.

"That's what we want to talk with you about," I said.

Our server approached to take our drink orders.

"Hi, Bobbie," I said. "Busy night, huh?"

"It's insane," she said, smiling. "Oh, and Chef Claire said you should just get started. She's swamped at the moment."

"Okay," I said, nodding. "She's already let us know what she wants to do."

Victor and Abby stared at me, confused, and as soon as Bobbie departed, I glanced back and forth at them.

"We need to talk about Wags."

"What about it?" Victor said.

"We want to sell it," I said as a simple statement of fact.

"Sell it?" Abby said, stunned. "Why on earth would you want to do that?"

"Because we don't enjoy what we're doing," Josie said.

"Have I done something to upset you?" Abby said.

"No, it's nothing like that," I said, patting her hand. "You're doing a fantastic job, and we love working with you. But we have no business being in the corporate world. And Wags deserves to have a board of directors fully committed to its growth and development."

"I'm sure we can figure out a way to make it work for you," Abby said. "I know you hate dealing with the finance side. And all the meetings."

"See, that's just it," I said. "That's the core business of the board. And the more time we spend doing it, the more we understand just how important all that stuff is. But I'm already dreading it. And I'm positive it's only going to get worse. It's just not fair to you or the company."

"I see," Abby whispered. "Wow, this is a total shock."

"It certainly is," Victor said, rubbing his forehead. "Do you have any idea how much money you'll be leaving on the table?"

"We do," my mother said. "But I'm sure we can figure out a way to minimize the pain."

Victor grinned at my mother.

"Do you now?" he said, laughing. "Let me guess. You want me to buy it, right?"

"Nothing gets past you, Victor," I said, feeling like a thousand-pound weight was beginning to lift. "You're obviously our preferred buyer."

"But we imagine that Dog World would be very interested as well," my mother said with a casual shrug.

I knew my mother was floating that possibility just to get Victor's attention. It did.

"You haven't been talking with them, have you?" he said, frowning.

"Not yet," my mother said, beaming at him. "So far, the only person we've spoken to is Gerald."

"Gerald? Who's Gerald?" Victor said.

Abby laughed.

"You are something else, Mrs. C.," she said, shaking her head.

"What am I missing?" Victor said.

"Gerald is one of Mrs. C.'s buddies down here," Abby said. "Who just happens to be the Finance Minister."

"The Cayman Finance Minister wants to buy a dog toy company?" Victor said, confused.

"No, he just has some interesting ideas about how we should sell it," my mother said, glancing up at our server who returned carrying a tray of drinks. "Thanks, Bobbie." She took a sip of wine, then folded her hands on the table and sat back in her chair.

"Okay, now I get it," Victor said, nodding. "Bringing in the Finance Minister to help you broker the deal is a bit over the top, but I'll play. Let's hear it."

"Fifteen million. And a hundred thousand shares of Middleton stock," I said.

"Ouch," Victor said. "Gerald's been busy."

"He's very good at what he does," my mother said.

"Yes, I imagine he is," Victor said. "Is that all?"

"No," I said. "You need to agree to a five-year contract for Abby as CEO."

"That won't be a problem," Victor said, squeezing Abby's hand. "Abby isn't going anywhere. And we'd be crazy not to have her running it."

"Perfect," I said. "And would you still plan on selling the food products Chef Claire has developed?"

"Of course," Victor said. "The initial tests have been off the charts."

"Then we'd like you to keep Chef Claire on retainer for the next five years as well. She'll keep developing new ideas and giving them to Abby."

"I don't have a problem with that," Victor said, shrugging as he took a sip of his drink. Then he rattled his ice cubes and grinned at me.

"Don't start," I said, laughing. "So, what do you think?"

"Are you kidding?" Victor said. "I think you're all nuts. No offense, but walking away from this thing is one of the dumbest ideas I've heard in years." He paused to take another sip and collect his thoughts. "But I should warn you that my board loves to negotiate and never accepts the initial asking price." He chuckled. "It makes them feel like they're earning their keep."

"Then tell your board we want twenty million and two hundred thousand shares," my mother said.

"You are something else," he said, laughing. "You know, we're about to have a vacant seat on our board. How would you like me to recommend you? You'd be great."

"That's very sweet of you, Victor," my mother said, beaming at him. "And normally I'd be very interested. But I'll have to pass. I'm going to be extremely busy the next several months."

"Doing what?" Victor said, raising an eyebrow.

"Why, planning a wedding, of course."

Chapter 10

After calling his office, I tracked Detective Renfro down the next morning eating breakfast at a funky beachfront joint not far from our place. He was halfway through his omelet when he noticed me trudging through the sand toward him, and, this time, didn't seem at all surprised to see me. He set his knife and fork down then raised his coffee mug and took a sip as he gestured at the empty seat on the other side of the two-seater table.

"Good morning, Suzy," he said, refocusing on his food. "Have you had breakfast yet?"

"I have," I said, giving his omelet a loving stare. "What's good here? I've driven by this place a hundred times but have never eaten here."

"It's all good," Detective Renfro said, stacking a chunk of the omelet onto a piece of flatbread. He gazed out at the ocean as he chewed his food. "It's going to be warm today."

"It is," I said, trying to decide if I was still hungry as a server approached. "Hi," I said to her. "Can I please get some coffee?"

"Of course," she said, smiling. "Do you need anything else, Detective?"

"No, I'm good. Thanks, Shandra."

The server poured my coffee then turned to leave but stopped when she heard my voice.

"Oh, and maybe I'll have an order of fruit," I said, quickly scanning the menu.

"Certainly," the server said, again starting to walk away.

"And an order of the flatbread. It looks delicious," I said.

"You know, if you add a couple of eggs, I can just bring you the breakfast special. It would save you a couple bucks," the server said as she topped off Detective Renfro's mug.

"Let's do that," I said, nodding. "Eggs over easy, please."

"You got it," she said, pausing a few seconds just to make sure I was done ordering before she headed off.

"More food for less money," I said. "You gotta love that."

"I thought you said you'd already eaten," Detective Renfro said.

"Ocean air always makes me hungry," I said, removing my sunglasses.

"Is that what I think it is?" he said, nodding at my engagement ring.

"It is," I said, holding my hand out.

"Congratulations," Detective Renfro said. "I'm very happy for you."

"He's a great guy," I said, beaming.

"And obviously very brave."

"Funny."

"So, what brings you here this morning?" he said, polishing off the last of his omelet.

"Oh, I was just in the neighborhood," I said, glancing out at the water. "And I thought I saw your car."

"It's amazing that you can pick my police car out of the dozen or so that are driving around," he said. "Especially since they're assigned randomly at the station."

"Then I guess I just got lucky," I said, flashing him a big smile.

"You want to talk about Jennifer Jensen, don't you?"

"Well, since you brought her up, sure," I said, splashing a bit of milk into my coffee.

"Suzy, what's it going to take before you believe me when I tell you that investigations like this are really none of your business?"

"Trick question, right?"

Detective Renfro exhaled loudly and stared out at a windsurfer who was expertly cutting in and out of the light chop not far from shore.

"C'mon, Detective," I said. "We're just talking. It's not like I'm planning to make an arrest. But I don't think Jennifer killed her parents."

"I'll make sure to let everyone on the force know that," the detective said, continuing to work his way through what was left of his breakfast. "It should save us a lot of time."

"She was estranged from them, but she's not a killer," I said.

"She's going to inherit a fortune."

"That doesn't make her a killer," I said.

"Maybe."

"You feel the same way, don't you?"

"Like I just said, it's none of your business. I can't talk about it. It's an ongoing investigation," he said, shaking his head before taking a sip of coffee.

"Then how about I just ask you some yes-no questions? That way, you're really not *talking* about it. You're merely *responding*."

"No."

"See? That wasn't so hard, was it?"

Despite being annoyed, the detective laughed.

"If I agree to humor you, will that shut you up?"

"I doubt it, but it's probably worth a shot."

Detective Renfro sat back in his chair and motioned for me to proceed.

"Cool," I said, leaning forward. "You don't believe the explosion was an accident, do you?"

"No."

"And Jennifer Jensen is your number one suspect, right?"

"Maybe."

"Maybe?"

"That's the best I can do at the moment," Detective Renfro said.

"That's okay, I can work with that," I said, sitting back as the server approached with my food. "Thanks. It looks great."

The server topped off both our coffees then departed. I tore off a piece of the flatbread, broke one of the eggs with it, then dredged it through the yoke. I savored the bite as I formulated my next question.

"Where are you guys at with the connection between the cocaine and the cockfights?"

"What makes you think there's a connection?" he said, frowning.

"It's a logical assumption," I said with a shrug. "This flatbread is amazing. Do they make it onsite?"

"I'm sure they do," the detective said. "Why is that a logical assumption?"

"Well, since this guy Jensen was an inveterate gambler with cash flow problems, my guess is that he must have owed money to some local people," I said, tossing my line in the water to see if I got a nibble.

"You did have a nice, long chat with the daughter, didn't you?"

"What can I say?" I said, smiling at him. "A lot of people like talking to me."

"I wonder what their secret is."

"It's a little early for snarky, Detective," I said, making a face at him. "Now, about the possible connection between the coke and the cockfighting."

"What about it?"

"How am I doing so far?"

"Keep talking," Detective Renfro said, nodding.

"Okay, I'm on the right track. So, if Jensen loved betting on cockfights as much as his daughter says, I can't help but wonder if at least one of the people he owed money to might be someone he was betting with at the local cockfighting events."

"You can't *help but wonder*?" the detective said, raising an eyebrow at me.

"It's what I do," I said, shrugging. "And judging by what we saw floating on the surface after the explosion, it's pretty clear that Jensen was bringing in a whole lot of coke."

"He was."

"Was he already on your radar as a drug smuggler?"

"He was not."

"Were you aware that he had a gambling problem?"

"Why would we know that?"

"Yeah, I get that," I said, frowning. "Especially since you guys let this barbaric cockfighting nonsense continue unabated. How *would* you know?"

Detective Renfro scowled but said nothing.

"And since cockfighting has been linked with drug dealers for a long time, I don't think it's much of a stretch to connect the two in this case. You know, two underworld activities coming together."

"Underworld?"

"Yeah, you know what I mean," I said, nodding. "Shady characters lurking in dark alleys, smoky backroom deals, stuff like that. It's not like Jensen would be unloading big bundles of cocaine in front of the government office buildings."

Detective Renfro flinched, and his eyes flared briefly, but long enough for me to catch it.

"What is it?" I said, leaning forward. "I just touched a nerve."

"No, you didn't," he said, glancing out at the ocean. "I just got a bit of a chill, that's all."

"It's 85 and climbing, Detective," I said, frowning at him. "You reacted when I mentioned the government offices. You think someone from the government might be involved?"

"I have no idea what you're talking about," Detective Renfro said. "And I really should get going."

I polished off the last of my eggs and flatbread and went to work on my fruit. I glanced over at him as I munched on a slice of mango.

"Relax, Detective," I said, wiping my mouth. "We're just talking here."

"Not anymore," he said, reaching for his wallet.

"No, breakfast is on me," I said, sliding another slice of mango into my mouth. "It's the least I can do."

"Please, try not to do *more*, Suzy," he said, getting to his feet. "Thanks for breakfast. I imagine I'll be seeing you around."

"I'm looking forward to it, Detective."

"I'm glad one of us is."

"Harsh," I said, laughing.

He shook his head and waved as he turned and headed toward his car. I watched him drive off, then stared out at the water as several thoughts began to churn and collide. I paid the bill, checked my watch, and decided that Gerald had probably arrived at his office by now.

Chapter 11

The security guard at the front desk of the Government Administration Building stared at my passport photo then glanced up at me and smiled. I frowned when I realized he recognized me from my last visit about a year ago.

"You're Gerald's friend, right? Welcome back," he said, handing me a visitor's badge. "How's that sunburn doing?"

"Just peachy, thanks," I said, making a beeline for the elevator that would take me to the fifth floor.

When the elevator came to a stop, I headed down the hall to Gerald's office. His executive assistant was sitting at her desk, and she recognized me immediately. She gave me the goofy grin I'd expected, and I approached the desk tentatively and waited for her to speak first.

"Suzy, right?" she said, cocking her head.

"That's me," I said, forcing a smile. "It's nice to see you again."

"Yes, it's been too long," she said, grinning. "Especially since your last visit was so...*memorable.*"

I waited out her laughter, quietly fuming. The last time, in fact, the only time I'd visited Gerald in his office I was dealing with the worst sunburn I'd ever gotten. And to help mitigate the pain, I'd been wearing loose-fitting clothing including a pair of baggy shorts that happened to fall around my ankles when I got up from the chair I'd been sitting in. After tripping over my shorts and falling to the floor on my hands and knees, his executive assistant had walked in and caught us in what she logically assumed was a very compromising position. The word of what she had seen, greatly embellished I'm sure by those telling the story, had spread like wildfire through the office after I made a hasty retreat out of the building.

"Is he in his office?" I said as casually as I could manage.

"He is," she said. "Is he expecting you?"

"No, he's not," I said.

"Let me buzz him and see if he can squeeze you in before his first meeting," she said, reaching for her phone. "Suzy Chandler is here to see you, sir. Of course. Thank you." She hung up and smiled at me. "Go right in. You'll have about fifteen minutes." Then she did her best not to laugh. "I hope that will be enough time," she said, unable to get the smile off her face.

"I'm sure it will," I said, biting my bottom lip.

"Can I bring you anything? Coffee? Tea? Maybe some sunscreen?"

"Funny," I said, heading for the door.

I knocked then entered the office. Gerald was sitting behind his desk reviewing a thick document.

"Suzy, what a nice surprise," he said, getting up and gesturing for me to sit in the same high-backed leather chair I'd been in before. "Nice shorts. I assume they fit a lot better than that other pair."

"Everybody's a comedian."

"What brings you here this beautiful morning?"

"I just had breakfast with Detective Renfro," I said.

"Sure, I know Renfro. He's a good cop," he said, nodding. "That's not exactly earth-shattering news, but it's your meeting. I'm sure I'll pick up the thread at some point."

"I was talking with him about Jennifer Jensen."

"Okay," he said, frowning. "And?"

"And she's the prime suspect at the moment," I said.

"Did Detective Renfro tell you that?" Gerald said, raising an eyebrow. "Because if he did, I might need to have a little chat with his superiors."

"No, she told me when I was at her place," I said, then decided to tell Gerald a small lie so as not to burn any bridges. "Detective Renfro didn't tell me anything."

"How's Jennifer doing?" Gerald said. "I haven't had a chance to talk with her yet."

"That's right," I said, nodding. "You mentioned that you knew her."

"I do," he said, glancing at his watch.

"How well?"

"How well do I know her?" Gerald said, annoyed. "That's none of your business, Suzy."

"Geez, Gerald, relax," I said, staring at him. "I'm just making chit-chat here."

"Did Jen say something to you?" Gerald said.

"About you? Not a word. Jen?" I said, then the penny dropped, and I grinned at him. "You old dog. You're sleeping with her, aren't you?"

Gerald stared off at a wall that displayed dozens of pictures of him posing with dignitaries and celebrities then shook his head and focused on me.

"Not anymore," he whispered. "We haven't spoken in months."

"You had a fight?"

"Yeah, a big one," he said.

"Can I ask what it was about?"

"No, you can't," he snapped.

"Fair enough. I always thought you were into blondes," I said, grinning at him. "I didn't know you had a thing for pink hair."

"It's pink?" he said, confused. "The last time I saw her it was bright green."

"That would have been when you had the big fight, right?"

Gerald exhaled loudly and shook his head at me.

"Tell me again why you're here. I'm having a hard time following."

I was about to explain then stopped. Since I'd already told him that Detective Renfro hadn't divulged anything, I couldn't mention his reaction to my offhand remark about Jensen selling drugs in front of the government offices. I decided to stay generic.

"I'm just trying to figure out if there is a connection between drug smuggling and cockfighting."

Gerald shook his head sadly and rubbed his eyes.

"Oh, Suzy. What am I going to do with you?"

"What would you like to do, Gerald?" I said with a big grin. "But I should probably tell you there's no way I'm dying my hair pink."

"Funny," he said. "I was thinking about something a bit more direct to get your attention. Like throwing you out my window. But your mother would never forgive me."

"So, what do you think?" I said.

"About a possible connection between those two activities?"

"Yeah."

"I think you need to stop worrying about it," Gerald said. "Leave the investigation to Detective Renfro and the rest of the people we pay to figure those things out."

"Sure, sure," I said, nodding. "I was just thinking, since cockfighting is such a despicable activity, it must attract some of the *seedier* people who live here."

"I'm sure it does," Gerald said. "But it's none of your business. Got it?"

"Have you ever been to one?"

"A cockfight?"

"Yeah."

"I have not," he said, shaking his head. "Like you, I think it's despicable."

"Then why don't you do something to shut it down?"

"Suzy, I'm about to go into a meeting with a guy from Brazil who wants to invest half a billion in Cayman. And after that, I'm going to a budget meeting where we're going to have to find a way to cut several million dollars without doing too much damage to the people who live here. I'm sorry, but cockfighting is way down my list of things to worry about."

"But you could make a few calls, right?"

"I could, but I won't," he said, glaring at me. "Just let the police handle it."

"Let me ask you a question, Gerald," I said, returning his glare.

"Why stop now?" he said, spreading his arms.

"If we were talking about dog fighting you'd do something to stop it, right?"

Gerald flinched like I'd punched him. He leaned forward and selected a piece of hard candy from the bowl on the coffee table between us. He held the bowl out, and I took one and began unwrapping it. Gerald continued to think about my question as he rolled the candy around in his mouth.

"Dog fighting? Yes, I certainly would," he said.

"I know you would." I said, popping the piece of candy into my mouth and immediately tasting cinnamon. "But I guess roosters don't make the cut, huh?"

"C'mon, Suzy, give me a break," Gerald said, crunching down hard.

"I just find it hard to believe-" I said, then choked as the piece of candy slid down my throat and got stuck. I gagged and tried to cough, but I couldn't catch my breath. I gasped for air and clawed at my throat.

"Are you okay?" Gerald said, hopping up from his chair.

"I...can't...breathe," I said, clutching my chest. "Hi...hi..."

"Heimlich?" Gerald said, pulling me out of my chair.

I could only manage a small nod. Gerald positioned me behind the leather chair, and I placed both hands on it. He stood behind me and wrapped both hands around my chest, and pulled hard. I continued to gag and gasp for breath, and he repeated the maneuver a second time. Then a third. Just as the piece of candy flew out of my mouth and across the office, Gerald's executive assistant knocked on the door and poked her head inside.

"Your ten o'clock is waiting for you in the conference room," she said, then stared at us and shook her head. "Oh, Gerald. Not again."

Chapter 12

I picked up the wet tennis ball that Chloe had dropped at my feet and tried to shield myself from the torrent of water she was shaking off. I grabbed my towel and wiped my face then glanced down at her.

"You did that on purpose, didn't you?" I said, laughing.

Chloe barked once and continued to stare at the tennis ball. I fired it into the deep end of the pool and watched as she raced after it then dove into the water. Captain and Polly were wrestling in the water over a chew toy and playfully growling at each other. I took a sip of my still cold beer and saw Rooster heading our way carrying a tray. Al and Dente, draped around Chef Claire's legs, went on point and stared at Rooster as he placed the tray on a table and sat down. The three of us, trailed by both Goldens, got up from our loungers and joined him.

"What do we have here?" Josie said, studying the collection of appetizers and small sandwiches.

"Pretty much a little bit of everything," Rooster said, selecting one of the sandwiches. "This is the pork roast that Chef Claire brought home from the restaurant. I toasted the baguette and hit it with some of that fig jam."

"You're hired," Chef Claire said, laughing. Then something caught her eye, and she waved at Henry who was walking up from the beach.

"Hey, Henry," Josie said. "You're just in time for a snack."

All three dogs clamored out of the pool to greet him and proceeded to shake all over him.

"Sorry about that, Henry," I said.

"Don't worry about it," he said, bending down to pet them. "It actually feels pretty good. I was wondering if I could borrow your hedge clippers. Mine just snapped in half."

"Sure, help yourself," I said. "They're in the garage."

He waved and headed off, and we turned our attention back to the nosh plate Rooster had put together. Henry reappeared a few moments later and approached the table. He bent down to say hello to Al and Dente then helped himself to one of the mini-sandwiches. He took a bite and nodded his approval.

"Say, Henry?" I said, taking a sip of my beer. "I've got a question for you."

"Your mother says I should be on guard every time you say that," he said, laughing.

"No, this is an easy one," I said. "Where would I find the local cockfight?"

"You want to go to a cockfight?" he said, frowning at me.

"Well, I don't really want to," I said, shrugging. "It's more like I have to."

"Someone is making you go to a cockfight?" he said, polishing off the last of his sandwich and reaching for another.

"It's more of a self-inflicted mandate," I said.

Josie and Chef Claire snorted.

"I don't think that's a good idea, Suzy," Henry said, sitting down in the empty chair next to mine.

"I'd be shocked if you did," I said, laughing.

"No, I'm serious," he said. "From what I hear, those things can get pretty rowdy."

"Save your breath, Henry," Josie said, building a nosh plate. "We've spent the last hour trying to talk her out of it."

"Does your mom know you're going?"

"No, and she doesn't need to know," I said, cocking my head at him. "Okay?"

"You can't go there by yourself, Suzy."

"Josie and Rooster are coming with me," I said.

Henry glanced at them, and they confirmed it with a nod.

"Okay," Henry said. "I really don't think it's a good idea. But I'll make a call."

"Who are you going to call?" I said.

"The guy that organizes them is an acquaintance of mine," Henry said, getting up from his chair.

"Acquaintance? He's not a friend?" I said.

"No, he's not. And if you happen to meet him, which I don't recommend, you'll know why." He grabbed a wedge of cheese from the tray. "I'll text you the directions. And try not to do anything stupid while you're there."

He waved and headed off, pausing long enough to say goodbye to all the dogs.

"Well, he certainly got my attention," Josie said.

90

"Me too," Rooster said.

"You think it might be dangerous?" Josie said.

"For the roosters?" I said. "I'm sure it will be."

"Good one," Josie said. "I think we should dress down for it. You know, so we'll blend in with the crowd."

"That's a great idea," I said.

"I may need a few fashion tips," Josie said, grinning at Chef Claire and Rooster. "Are you sure you can't join us?"

"No, there's another cruise ship coming in tomorrow," Chef Claire said. "The restaurant is going to be jammed."

"You're working way too hard," Josie said.

"Tell me about it," she said. "I'm thinking about hiring another sous chef."

"Go for it," I said.

"It would put a dent in our margin," Chef Claire said.

"So what?" Josie said. "You're about to become independently wealthy."

"That's right. I am," she said, smiling as she raised her beer in a toast. "To my new horse."

"You're gonna buy a horse?" Josie said.

"I am," she said, nodding. "And since you guys are about to open a rescue program right behind the Inn, I'll have a place to keep it."

"A horse?" Josie said, nodding. "Nice." Then she frowned.

"What's the matter?" I said.

"I'm just thinking about us going to the cockfight."

"Are you worried?" I said.

"Actually, I am getting a weird vibe about going," Josie said.

"Well, why don't we check with our expert?" I said, laughing. "Polly. Come here, girl."

"Don't start," Josie said, shaking her head.

"No, this should be good," I said, reaching down to pet the poodle. "She's such a good girl. What a good girl."

"You're so weird," Josie said.

"Polly, we're going to go to a cockfight. A cockfight. What do you think about that?"

The poodle stared up at me, then nudged my arm and barked loudly. Then she nudged my arm again and sat down on my feet. I stared at the dog, then glanced around the table.

"Wow," I said, confused. "That's odd. She probably knows the word because her owner used to go all the time, right?"

Josie and Rooster frowned at the dog, then at each other.

"That must be it," I said, then focused on the dog. "What's the matter, Polly? Don't you think we should go to the cockfight?"

The dog barked again and nuzzled my leg. But she remained solidly planted on my feet.

"She's freaking me out," Josie said.

"I'm sure it's just a coincidence," I said, rubbing the dog's head. "Right?"

Chapter 13

I turned left off Eastern Avenue and gripped the steering wheel tight as I waited for Josie's next instruction. I glanced through the rearview mirror into the backseat of the jeep where Rooster was keeping a watchful eye on our surroundings.

"It's certainly a different world over here," he said.

"Henry said to be prepared for the neighborhood," I said. "He said it can be a little sketchy."

"Well, I doubt if we're going to find cockfighting at the Ritz-Carlton," Josie said. "Make your next right."

I slowed down and made the turn. The neighborhood changed again, and I saw several makeshift houses bathed in dim light.

"Henry said that after the last major hurricane, a lot of people just rebuilt from scrap materials they found scattered around," I said. "Wow, this is a tough way to live."

"I think Gerald should make some housing money available," Josie said. "After all, he is the Finance Minister. You should say something the next time you visit him."

"Oh, I'm never going back to his office," I said, shaking my head.

"Just because a cinnamon ball tried to kill you?" Josie said, laughing. "Make a right just after the house with the red door."

"Why doesn't anybody use actual street addresses down here?" I said. "It would make things a whole lot easier."

I made the turn and headed down a dark street. I slowed to a crawl and glanced around.

"Maybe Polly was right," I said. "Did you see the way she tugged at my leg before we left tonight?"

"I don't want to talk about it," Rooster said. "That dog is really starting to freak me out."

"Tell me about it," Josie said. "Okay, we're close. Henry's directions say to keep going until you see two streetlights directly across the street from each other."

"There they are. About a hundred feet dead ahead," I said, surprised. "I guess I can park anywhere, right?"

Josie shrugged, and I came to a stop. We climbed out of the jeep and huddled under the streetlamp on our side of the street. Josie held the directions out so we could read them.

"Yellow house with a dirt path on the right side," Rooster said, glancing around.

"There it is," Josie said, pointing at the dilapidated structure. "Okay, let's get this over with."

We slowly headed for the path, huddling inches apart as we walked. My head was on a swivel as my stomach churned, and I wondered momentarily if I'd finally lost my mind. It was ten o'clock at night, and instead of lounging by the pool with the dogs before heading off to get a good night's sleep, I was walking down an unlit dirt path about to watch armed roosters battle to the death.

We soon heard the muffled sounds of loud voices and excited chatter. At the end of the path, a large man smoking a cigarette was leaning against a door. The makeshift structure was quite large, perhaps even a bit bigger than the house, and a solitary lightbulb hung above the door. The man crushed his cigarette out with his foot and gave us the once-over. He continued to stare at us as we approached.

"Hi," I said with a big smile. "We're here for the cockfight."

"Cockfight?" he said, folding his arms across his chest. "I don't know what you're talking about. We're playing bingo."

"Our friend Henry spoke with Ramon earlier today," I said.

"Good for Henry," the man said, refusing to budge from in front of the door.

"Oh, hang on a sec," Josie said, removing Henry's directions from the pocket of her jeans. "I forgot. Henry said we might need the code."

"Code?" I said, frowning.

"B12," Josie said to the man.

"Bingo. That's the one," the man said as he took a few steps away from the door. "That'll be ten bucks each."

I dug the money out of my jeans and handed it over.

"Enjoy your evening. We have six fights on the card tonight."

We headed inside and remained in the doorway as we took a good look around. In the center of the dirt floor was a circular ring about twelve-feet wide separated from the rest of the cramped space by a plywood barrier about three feet high. Spectators ringed the barrier and were stacked six deep. I estimated that there were over a hundred people in attendance. A thick cloud of smoke hung over the room, and the pungent scent of cheap cigars filled my nostrils and reminded me of ammonia. At least, I was pretty sure the ammonia smell was coming from the cigars. It certainly hadn't been used as a cleaning product. The ring was empty, but the anticipation was building, and I watched a bald man waddle his way through a set of black curtains then step into the ring. His torso was way too big for his legs, and he was sweating profusely with a stubby cigar wedged between his teeth. Two large gold hoops hung from his ears, and he paused to scratch himself before he welcomed everyone and informed us that the first bout would begin in five minutes. Then he waddled back through the curtains.

"That must be Ramon," Josie said.

"Good guess," I said, glancing around. "Look at all the money people are holding."

"Big money," Rooster said, nodding as took in the surroundings. "Where do you want to stand?"

"Someplace where we can get a good look at who's here," I said.

"And a place where we won't be able to see the fights," Josie said. "This is disgusting."

"No argument there." Rooster said, pointing at the other side of the room near the black curtains that separated the audience from the area where I assumed the roosters and their handlers were waiting.

We slowly worked our way through the crowd, drew only a few quizzical looks, and came to a stop directly in front of the curtains.

"They have a beer vendor," Rooster said, shaking his head. "Nothing like knocking back a couple of cold ones while you watch some roosters hack themselves to death."

"That's enough, Rooster. I don't need a play by play announcer," Josie said, surveying the scene. "But let me know if you spot anybody selling snacks."

I continued to scan the crowd, then flinched when my eyes landed on a group of people standing near the ring on the opposite side from us.

"What is it?" Josie said.

"Those are the folks I saw at Jennifer Jensen's place," I said, focusing on the couple I had spoken with by the pool. "That's interesting."

"And they look like they're ready to do some serious betting," Rooster said.

Then I flinched again when my eyes landed on another familiar face. I used both elbows to nudge Rooster and Josie, and they followed my eyes.

"How about that?" Josie said.

"What the heck is he doing here?"

My eyes narrowed as I glared at Gerald who was wearing a floppy hat and sunglasses along with a nondescript work shirt and khaki pants. But even though he was doing his best to look like a gardener, I recognized him immediately. He was chatting quietly with a young man, and they were both sipping beers.

"Never been to a cockfight before, huh? Gerald lied to me. Why would he do that?"

"That's a very good question," Josie said. "Do you know who he's with?"

"No, I've never seen him before."

"Do you want to go over and have a chat with him?"

"No, in fact, I hope he doesn't even notice we're here," I said. "I'd like to figure out what he's up to. The little liar."

Ramon appeared through the curtains trailed by two men who were each carrying a small cage with a rooster inside. They opened a gate in the plywood barrier and entered the ring. Ramon announced the two contestants as the men opened the cages then held their roosters and stroked their feathers as they armed the birds. A few moments later, the glint of metal blades attached to the roosters' feet got the crowd buzzing even louder, and stacks of cash began changing hands. I felt my stomach churn again.

"This is sick," I said as all three men left the ring.

"That's the word for it," Josie said, staring into the ring as the roosters slowly approached each other.

Then the two roosters bounced into each other, and one of the birds hopped into the air kicking its legs and landed a blow on the other rooster's chest. A red patch quickly began forming on top of the bird's feathers.

"That poor thing. We gotta stop this," I whispered.

"How the heck are we going to do that?" Rooster said, frowning at me.

"We need a diversion," I said.

"Like what?" Rooster said.

"We need something that will make them all leave," I said. "And not come back."

"Cockfighting is illegal, right?" Josie said.

"It certainly is," I said. "But from what Gerald and Detective Renfro told me, the cops don't seem to care."

"Yes," Josie said, with an evil grin. "But these people don't know that."

Rooster and I beamed at Josie.

"You're so good," I said, giving her a hug. Then I looked at Rooster. "You should do it. You've got that big, deep voice.

"My pleasure," Rooster said, glancing around. Then he wrapped himself in one of the curtains and disappeared from sight. "You ready?"

"Go for it," I said, inching closer to the curtain.

"This is the police! Nobody move! This is a raid!"

Cries of surprise followed by nervous chatter ensued, then everyone in the room made a beeline for the exits. We stood back to watch, and several people brushed against us as they hurriedly made their way through the curtains. Soon, the area surrounding the ring was empty, and I peeked through the curtains and realized that everyone had also cleared out of the back room. But they had left the roosters behind.

"Come on, let's go," I said, tugging both their sleeves.

"Where are we going?" Josie said, confused.

"To do some rooster rescue," I said, stepping into the back room.

I glanced around and noticed the remaining ten roosters standing in their own small cages. Josie and Rooster both frowned.

"There's no way we can carry all these cages," Josie said.

"But we can carry two each," I said. "We can double up on some of them. Two roosters to a cage."

"I doubt if they're going to like that," Josie said.

"Probably not," I said, opening one of the cages and grabbing a very surprised bird that kicked his legs and voiced his

100

displeasure. "But it sure beats the alternative they're looking at. C'mon. Hurry up."

"When you're right, you're right," Josie said, reaching into another cage. "Ow, the little bugger bit me."

"Don't you mean pecked?"

"Don't nitpick," Josie said.

Rooster grabbed two of the cages and glanced around.

"How are we going to get out of here?" he said.

"We'll go out the back," I said, grabbing two cages. "Then we'll work our way up the path and head for the jeep."

"I don't like this," Rooster said, heading for the door.

"C'mon, we gotta hurry," I said, struggling with the cages that were bouncing off my knees. "They'll be coming back for their birds."

"I doubt if anybody is coming back soon," Rooster said. "Did you see the way Gerald hightailed it out of there?"

"The Finance Minister at a cockfight," Josie said, laughing. "That's a page one story."

We stepped outside into darkness and stood quietly for a moment listening.

"Okay, I think the coast is clear," I said, doing my best lumber as I headed for the dirt path. The cages continued to bang off my knees, and by the time I reached the street, I was dealing with a two-legged limp. "Rooster, let's stack the cages in the back seat. And you might have to hold them."

"I'll figure something out," he said, placing the two cages he was carrying on the floor of the jeep.

As soon as he had all six cages in some semblance of order, he hunched down on his knees with his back facing us. He placed his hands on top of the other four cages stacked on the seat to hold them steady.

"How are the roosters doing?" I said, starting the engine.

"They seem a little confused at the moment," Rooster said.

"Join the club," Josie said. "Let's get out of here."

"Where to?" I said.

"I'm thinking the rescue center," Josie said.

"Oh, good call," I said, turning the jeep around and accelerating. "You got your keys with you?"

"I do," she said. "We can put them in the aviary with the other birds. If anybody asks where they came from, we'll just tell them they were dropped off in the middle of the night."

"Which, technically, wouldn't be a lie," I said, grinning at her.

"How many laws do you think we've broken tonight?" Rooster said over his shoulder.

"Let's hope we never get the chance to find out," Josie said, glancing into the backseat.

Chapter 14

I came to a stop in front of the rescue center, and Josie raced up the front steps to unlock the door. Then she ran back to the jeep and helped Rooster and I carry the six cages inside. I closed and locked the door and flipped the lights on.

"After we put them in the aviary, what should we do with the cages?" Josie said.

"We'll just put them in the storage area for now," I said. "Maybe Teresa can use them for something."

The adrenaline rush all three of us experienced during what Josie would soon come to call the Reckless Red Rooster Robbery had begun to wane, and we took our time getting them settled inside the netted aviary behind the facility. The roosters wandered around and seemed to be grumbling to each other as their claws kicked up small clouds of dust and dirt. We closed the aviary door, put the cages away, then regrouped in the registration area.

"The next time you organize a night out, how about we just stick with a movie?" Josie said, sitting down.

"What do you think Gerald was doing there?" I said, grabbing a fresh bag of bite-sized from a desk drawer and ripping it open.

"Trying to win some money would be my guess," Rooster said, waving off my offer of the bag.

"Tell me about the other people you saw there. The ones you met at the daughter's place," Josie said, grabbing a small handful.

"I only met two of them," I said. "They were drinking beer and smoking weed by the pool. The other three never got out of the water while I was there."

"Beer and weed? You went over there first thing in the morning," Josie said, popping one of the bite-sized.

"I did," I said. "But that didn't seem to matter to them. It was party central."

"They're friends of Jensen's daughter?" Rooster said.

"No, Jennifer said they all worked for her dad's company," I said. "She made it pretty clear she wasn't fond of having them around. Vultures was the term she used."

"Okay, that might be worth looking into," Josie said. "If we buy the connection between the drugs and the cockfighting."

"Do you believe there is?" I said.

"Suzy, I just spent the last hour kidnapping a bunch of roosters from a cockfight," she said, laughing. "At the moment, I'll believe anything."

I flashed back to my breakfast conversation with Detective Renfro, and his reaction to my offhand comment about Jensen selling drugs at the government offices again started rolling around my head. I scowled when an idea bubbled up to the surface.

"What's the matter?" Josie said, reacting to the look on my face.

"I'm just wondering if Gerald is somehow involved in all this," I said.

"Please, don't go there, Suzy," Josie said, grabbing another handful of the bite-sized. "Gerald's a lot of things, and I imagine he's not shy about cutting some corners from time to time. But I don't see him getting involved in drug smuggling."

"Would you have ever imagined seeing him at a cockfight?"

"No," she said after a long silence. "That was way out of character for him." Then she laughed. "But I'm sure you'll figure out a way to annoy it out of him."

"Gerald's the least of our problems at the moment," Rooster said, glancing out the window.

"What?" I said, getting up to look out the window. "Uh-oh."

"What is it?" Josie said, craning her neck to get a peek outside.

"Cops," Rooster said. "This is not good."

"Maybe we can pretend we're not here," I said.

"Suzy, the lights are on, and our jeep is parked right outside the front door," Rooster said, heading for the front door and opening it. "Good evening, Officers."

Two large uniformed policemen strolled inside and glanced around.

"Good evening," the larger of the two cops said. "I'm Officer Jones. And this is Officer Abbott."

"Nice to meet you," I said, beaming at them. "If you're looking to adopt, we don't open until nine."

"Don't start," Josie whispered.

"No, that's not why we stopped by," Officer Jones said, giving me a dead-eyed stare. "We're here about some roosters."

"I think you're in luck," I said. "We just got a bunch in earlier today. It's kind of an odd bird to have as a pet, but whatever floats your boat, right, Officer?"

"Suzy, I swear I'm going to knock you into next week if you don't stop," Josie whispered as she grabbed my hand and squeezed hard.

"Ow," I said, jerking my hand away.

"No, Ms. Chandler," Officer Jones said. "We're not here to adopt."

I frowned. The cop already knew my name. That probably wasn't a good sign.

"We're here about some stolen roosters," Officer Jones said, glancing around again.

"Why would anybody want to steal roosters?" I said, going for bewildered.

"That's a question we hope you'll be able to answer, Ms. Chandler," Officer Jones said.

"How do you know my name?"

"We just came from your mother's place."

"You've been talking to my mother?" I said, frowning.

"We have."

"Oh, that's not good," I said out loud to myself. Then I brightened. "Well, I wouldn't put too much stock in what she has to say, Officer. She's a bit of a drinker."

I flashed him my best smile that failed to connect.

"Knock...it...off," Josie whispered through clenched teeth.

"What did my mother have to say?"

"After she calmed down, she suggested that we might find you here," Officer Jones said. "This is your rescue center, isn't it?"

"Yes, Josie and I are the primary owners," I said, nodding.

"Feel free to leave me out of it," Josie said.

"What makes you think we were somehow involved in stealing roosters?" I said, offering the cops the bag of bite-sized they both waved away.

"Primarily, this," Officer Jones said, stepping closer to hold out his phone. "This was emailed to us earlier."

I stared at the photo on his phone and saw the back of our jeep with the license plate prominently displayed. Also in the photo was Rooster facing the camera with his arms spread on top of the cages stacked in the back seat.

"Probably not a photo you'll want on the mantel," Josie said, staring at the officer's phone.

"Yeah, probably not," Rooster said. "But it might make one hell of a Christmas card."

107

"Wishing you a cage-free Christmas?" Josie said, grinning at him.

"That's not bad," Rooster said, chuckling. "But I'll see if I can do better with my mug shot."

"Maybe we were just transporting some cages," I said. "We go through a ton of them around here."

"Ms. Chandler, please," Officer Jones said. "Don't insult our intelligence."

"I wouldn't think of doing that, Officer," I said. "It's just that I don't see any roosters in that photo."

"Okay," Officer Jones said, nodding. "If you don't mind, we're going to take a look around."

"You got a warrant?" I snapped.

"You got a death wish?" Josie whispered.

"No, we don't have a warrant," Officer Jones said. "But we do have probable cause."

"Probable?" I said, raising an eyebrow. "So, you're not certain it was us."

"Suzy, that's enough," Rooster said. "Let the officers do their job."

"No, Rooster," I said, taking a few steps back until I was blocking the doorway that led out back. "They just can't come in here and start rummaging around through the place."

"Ms. Chandler," Officer Jones said. "You're really starting to test my patience."

"Right back at you, Officer," I said. "I'm afraid I'm going to have to say no until you get a warrant to search the place."

"Okay, that's it," Officer Jones said, removing a pair of handcuffs from his belt. "I'm placing you under arrest."

"On what charge?"

"I'll let you know when I'm done writing them all down," he said, reaching for one of my arms.

I pulled my arm back, let loose with a string of expletives I didn't know I had in me, then dropped to one knee in serious pain when Officer Jones twisted my arms behind my back and expertly snapped the cuffs on. He pulled me to my feet and gently shoved me to get my walk to the police car started.

"Don't push me," I said, stumbling slightly as I took my first step. Then I glanced back and forth at Rooster and Josie. "You saw that, right? He shoved me. That's police brutality."

"Trust me, Ms. Chandler," Officer Jones said. "That wouldn't even register on the brutality scale. And let's hope I don't need to demonstrate that to you."

"Unbelievable," I said, then glared at the other cop. "Do you even know how to speak, Officer Silent?"

Officer Abbott merely shook his head in disbelief and held the front door open. Officer Jones continued to hold my handcuffed hands tight as he looked at Rooster and Josie.

"Can you two manage to walk quietly and get in the car, or am I going to have to cuff you as well?"

Josie and Rooster slowly made their way outside and climbed into the back seat and watched as I did my best perp-walk down the steps.

Chapter 15

Detective Renfro sat quietly until he was sure I had finished telling my version of the story, then closed his notebook and slid it to one side. I rubbed my wrists and yawned then focused on the detective.

"Do you have anything to add?" he said to Josie.

"No," she said. "But I do have one question."

"What's that?" the detective said.

"Do you guys have a bus I could borrow?"

"Funny," I said, glaring at her. "You're a big help."

"You don't need any help," she said. "Unless we're talking about therapy."

"Okay, you two. That's enough," Detective Renfro said. "I just have a couple of follow up questions."

"Go right ahead," I said, shrugging.

"Are you out of your freaking mind?" he said, staring at me.

"Good one, Detective," Josie said, then turned to me. "I didn't expect him to lead with rhetorical."

"We were merely doing your job for you, Detective," I said, fuming.

"Sure," Josie said, shaking her head. "Let's just insult the entire police force and get it over with."

"I'm serious," I snapped, then focused on the detective. "You and every other cop on the island know there's illegal cockfighting going on, but you don't do anything to shut it down."

"We have our reasons," Detective Renfro said, barely above a whisper.

I let his comment marinate for several seconds, then I grinned at him.

"I knew it," I said. "There is a connection between the drug smuggling and the cockfighting, isn't there?"

"I didn't say that," the detective said. "I merely said we have our reasons."

"Which are?" I said, cocking my head at him.

"Which are none of your business," he said with a small smile. Then his phone chirped, and he answered the call. "Renfro…That's fine. I'm done with them for the moment." He ended the call and placed his hands on the table. "Okay, I will leave you two for the time being. There are some other people who want to ask you a few questions."

"Great," I said, scowling. "We're gonna be here all night."

"Oh, let's hope so," he said, giving us a finger wave as he got up and headed for the door.

"He's not as funny as he thinks he is," I said, then glanced at Josie. "I'm sorry I got you into this mess."

"Yeah, I know you are," she said, nodding.

"You still mad at me?"

Josie reached out and slugged me hard on the arm.

"Maybe a little," she said, glancing around the room. "I need to pee."

"Can you hold it until they put us in the cell?" I deadpanned, then grinned at her.

"What the heck am I gonna do with you?"

"Well, you're going to start by being my maid of honor," I said.

"I thought you'd never ask."

"I didn't think I even needed to ask," I said, shrugging.

"And I assume you want a bachelorette party?"

"Of course," I said. "I'm thinking Montreal."

"We go to Montreal all the time," Josie said. "I'm thinking Vegas."

"That could work," I said. "Lots of good restaurants, catch a couple of shows, do some gambling."

"Maybe take in a cockfight," Josie said. "If you promise to behave yourself."

"Yeah, I'll see what I can do," I said. "Do you think they have cockfighting in Vegas?"

"I don't know," she said, shrugging. "Apparently, what happens in Vegas, stays there."

I laughed and gave her a hug, then we both turned when the door opened. A freshly showered Gerald entered and stared at us. He was wearing shorts and sandals and his usual short sleeved shirt with a flower pattern.

"What are you doing here?" I said.

"Great minds think alike," he said, sitting down across from us. "I was going to ask you the same thing." He draped a leg over his knee and glanced around the room. "We gave them the money to build this annex, but it's the first time I've actually been inside. It's not bad. As far as interrogation rooms go."

"What are you doing here, Gerald?"

"Trying to keep your butts out of jail, what else?" he said, shrugging.

"But how did you know we were here?" I said.

"Your mother called me."

"And she asked you to come down here?"

"Actually, she asked me to come with her," Gerald said, yawning.

"My mother's here?" I said, frowning.

"She is. She went to freshen up first."

"Crap. How mad is she?"

"I'm gonna go with volcanic," he said. "You know, molten lava."

"Got it. Don't worry, I'm sure I'll be able to talk her down off the ledge."

"Suzy, I don't think you understand," Gerald said, turning fatherly. "All three of you are facing some very serious charges."

"That's right," I said, glancing at Josie. "I completely forgot about Rooster. Is he okay?"

"He's fine," Gerald said. "Actually, he's in the room right next door."

"Are the cops threatening him with the same charges?"

"Well, you're the only one who's being charged with assaulting a police officer. I can't believe you bit a cop."

"He had his hands all over me," I said.

"Save it," he said, raising his hands. "But in addition to the other charges, Rooster is also looking at inciting a public riot and impersonating a police officer." He shook his head sadly. "Not good."

The door opened, and my mother stood in the doorway giving me a dark stare. Then she slowly walked across the room taking measured steps. Give her a cowboy hat and a six-shooter strapped around the waist, and she'd be right at home in a Sergio Leone western. She sat down next to Gerald and continued to glare at me but remained silent. I took her silence as a very bad sign.

"Hi, Mom," I said eventually.

"Young lady."

It was never good when she led with a young lady. I sat back in my chair and got ready for the barrage I knew was coming.

"I'd like an explanation," my mother said.

"Well, you see, Mom," I said, then stopped when she raised a hand to cut me off.

"I'd like to hear it from Josie."

I nodded and fell silent. Josie glanced at me then started talking. My mother and Gerald listened in silence, nodding and raising their eyebrows occasionally as she made her way through the story. When she got to the point of us being escorted into the room by the arresting officers, Josie stopped talking and leaned forward with her elbows on her knees as she waited for questions.

"Henry gave you directions to the cockfight?" my mother said.

"He did," Josie said.

"But I made him do it," I said. "So, there's no reason to be mad at him, Mom."

"I don't think you're in any position to tell me who I can be mad at, young lady."

"Just get it over with, Mom," I said. "Start blasting away, and then we'll move on with our lives, okay?"

"Oh, don't worry. I'll be blasting," she said. "And I'm going to start just as soon as I can convince the authorities that, while your actions tonight were beyond the pale, there's no reason to deport you."

"Deportation?" Josie whispered.

"Yes," my mother said.

Gerald nodded when I looked at him for confirmation.

"All we did was save some helpless roosters from certain death," I said, deciding I wasn't going down without a fight.

116

"Maybe we were a bit over the top, but it's not like we had a lot of options."

"A bit over the top?" my mother said. "You almost caused a public riot, and people could have been seriously hurt. And you called a police officer every name in the book."

"It was just some choice words I learned from you," I said, shrugging.

"Don't worry, I've got a few new ones I'm sure I'll be using on you later," she said. "And then you bit him?"

"Just on the hand," I said. "And he was such a big baby about it. *Oh, she bit me. I can't believe she bit me.* I'm surprised he didn't call in an officer down."

My mother took several deep breaths, appeared to be on the verge of hyperventilating, then exhaled audibly.

"I'll deal with you later," she said, then turned to Gerald. "Where do we go from here?"

"I'm sure we'll be able to post bail," he said. "But I have no idea if they'll decide to go ahead and formally press charges."

"Oh, I doubt if they'll press charges," I whispered.

"Do you now?" my mother said.

"Yes, they won't want the bad publicity," I said.

"I doubt if the police will worry about bad publicity from the arrest of a lunatic charged with stealing roosters," my mother said.

"No, probably not," I said. "But they might be worried about the press getting hold of how the police didn't do anything

117

to break up an illegal cockfighting operation they knew existed. Not to mention the word getting out about some of the people who were there tonight."

"Like who?" she said.

"Whom."

"Geez, Suzy. I'm beginning to think you do have a death wish," Josie said, shaking her head. "Don't start."

"Fine. Like whom?" my mother said, glaring at me.

"Like the Finance Minister," I whispered.

Gerald twitched in his chair, and my mother slowly turned to look at him.

"What?" my mother said. "You were there?"

"Yes," Gerald said, staring in disbelief at me. "I was there."

"So, you're not a fan of cockfighting, huh, Gerald?" I said. "By the way, nice outfit you were wearing. And if you are moonlighting as a gardener, our lawn could use a trim."

Gerald pursed his lips and shifted in his chair.

"Gerald, what were you doing there?" my mother said. "We've always agreed how barbaric it is."

"It is," he said with a sigh. "I have my reasons."

"Good enough reasons to want to keep it out of the papers?" I said.

Gerald got to his feet and shook his head.

"You really can be very annoying, Suzy."

"Yeah, I need to start working on that."

118

"Let me go have a chat with Detective Rollins," he said, heading for the door.

"Just like that?" my mother said, bewildered.

"Yeah," Gerald said, pausing at the door to look back at us. "Just like that."

"There you go. Problem solved," I said, glancing back and forth at my mother and Josie.

"I'm afraid not, young lady," she said. "Your problems are far from over."

"C'mon, Mom," I said, giving her a hug she eventually returned. "No harm, no foul. And we even managed to save the lives of some roosters in the process."

"Good for the roosters," she said, the air now taken out of her anger.

"Oh, and Josie has agreed to be my maid of honor. We're thinking about doing the bachelorette party in Vegas."

"Vegas? That could work," she said, nodding.

"Have you given any thought to who might be interested in giving me away?"

"I'm sure I'll have a long list of volunteers," she said, glaring at me.

"Oh, good one, Mom," I said. "It's nice to see you've got your sense of humor back."

"Don't push it, young lady."

Chapter 16

Given the lack of sleep, combined with our desire to keep a low profile for the next few days, we spent the morning lounging by the pool with the dogs. I checked in with Max, which only made me miss him even more, and was crushed when he told me that he would be away for at least another two weeks. I slid my phone into my bag and spent the next several minutes feeling sorry for myself. While I pouted, I watched the dogs roughhouse in the pool until they wore themselves out and settled down underneath the overhead misting system that lowered the external temperature on the verandah about twenty degrees.

Polly, who had been excited and almost seemed surprised to see us when we finally arrived home a little after three in the morning, was now sleeping between Al and Dente while Captain and Chloe were, as usual, curled together in a large, furry ball with one of the Newfie's front paws draped over the Aussie shepherd's back.

"They have a pretty good life, don't they?" Josie said as she studied the sprawled dogs.

"It's certainly better than the roosters," I said. "Teresa called a few minutes ago to tell us the cops swung by this morning."

"To return the birds to their owners?" Josie said.

"No, they want her to let them know if anybody stops by to claim them," I said. "All of a sudden, they're interested in shutting down the cockfighting operation. I guess there's nothing like the threat of a political scandal to get people's attention."

"Well, maybe we did end up doing some good after all," Josie said, her eyes wandering to the ocean-side section of the fence that ringed our property. The gate that led down to the beach opened, and she nudged me to get my attention.

"What's he doing here?" I said, watching as Gerald made his way toward us.

"Probably covering his tracks," Josie said. "Good afternoon, Gerald. How goes the war?"

"Josie," he said, beaming at her. "Hello, Suzy. What are you two up to today?"

"Just enjoying our new-found freedom," I said, pushing the chair next to me back from the table with my bare foot. "Since you came up from the beach, I guess that means you've been at my mom's place."

"I have," Gerald said, glancing around the lawn. "You're right, it does need cutting."

"Knock yourself out," Josie said, laughing. "The mower's in the garage."

"How's my mom's mood today?"

"Dark is the word that comes to mind," he said with a shrug. "When I left she was still railing at Rooster and Henry for

121

agreeing to play along with what she's calling your latest *descent into madness*. I had to get out of there for a while."

"Good call about us keeping our distance today," I said, glancing over at Josie. "Why aren't you at work?"

"It's Saturday," he said, sitting down and helping himself to some fruit and cheese.

"That's right," I said. "I completely forgot it was the weekend."

"Extended periods in jail can cause severe time distortion," Gerald said, waving to Chef Claire who was heading our way carrying a tray of sandwiches. "I believe the doctors call it dyschronometria."

"Good for the doctors," I said, making a face at him. "Do you need to talk to us about something, or did you just come for the free lunch?"

"Both," he said, getting up to offer Chef Claire his seat. He gave her a quick hug, grabbed another chair then sat back down and selected one of the sandwiches. "I assume you noticed that I wasn't alone last night."

"We noticed," Josie said.

"Thanks for not mentioning it at the police station last night," Gerald said, taking a big bite of his sandwich and nodding his approval.

"The thought didn't even cross my mind. In fact, I'd completely forgotten about it," I said, frowning. "Does it matter who you were there with?"

"It could," Gerald said, pouring himself a glass of iced tea.

"Who was he?" Josie said.

"That was William," Gerald said, refocusing on his sandwich. Then he glanced around at us and shrugged. "He's the Premier's son."

"You took the Premier's son to an illegal cockfight? Your *boss's* son?" I said, baffled. "Are you out of your mind?"

"Now you understand why I'm grateful you didn't mention it to the cops," he said.

"The press would have a field day with that," Josie said.

"Indeed," Gerald said, taking a long swig of tea. "But I didn't take him with me. I met him there."

"Does that make a difference?" I said. "Great sandwich, Chef Claire."

"Thanks," she said, making a racket as she bit into the end piece of the baguette and sprayed breadcrumbs in several directions. "I call it the Cayman Cheesesteak."

"William asked me to meet him there because he was worried about his safety." Gerald said.

"Okay," I said, leaning forward. "You have my undivided attention."

"Mine too," Josie said.

"William has made some bad choices in his life," Gerald said.

"Like going to cockfights?" I said.

"Unfortunately, that bad choice is way down the list," he said, taking a big bite of his sandwich. "William wasn't as interested in the cockfight as he was in seeing who else might have been there last night."

"Like the people who have him worried about his safety?" I said.

"Yes."

I sat back and waited for my thoughts to unscramble and eventually coalesce. But nothing solidified, and I frowned across the table at him.

"I guess my first question is why are you telling us all this?" I said. "A couple of minutes ago, you were thanking us for not mentioning it. Now, you want to talk about it?"

"As much as I hate saying this, I need your help," Gerald said casually as he picked at an imaginary piece of lint on his shirt. "Actually, it's William who needs your help. But I will be eternally grateful if there's anything you can do. He's my godson."

"Why isn't his father helping him?" I said. "After all, the guy is the head of the government down here."

"I was wondering the same thing," Josie said.

"This isn't something William can talk to his father about," Gerald said.

"Because of what he's doing or what it might do to his father's reputation if it got out?" I said.

"Possibly a whole lot of both," Gerald said.

"So, you're saying that William *is* doing something he shouldn't?" I said, rubbing my forehead.

"He says no," Gerald said. "But I'm not sure."

"And you don't feel comfortable talking to his dad about it?" I said.

"I promised William I wouldn't. At least for the time being."

I sat back and folded my arms across my chest, confused and struggling to piece together a thread I could follow.

"Gerald, given your reputation as an animal lover and advocate, I can see why you wouldn't want the word to leak that you were at a cockfight. But I can't see how it could do any real damage to the Premier."

"No, it wouldn't," Gerald said.

"So, it's got nothing to do with the cockfight," I said, shrugging. "You and William are worried that, if whatever this thing that he might be involved in gets leaked or attracts the attention of the cops, it could do some real damage to the Premier."

"Yes," Gerald said. "And I'm afraid it's already attracted the attention of the police."

I processed his last comment then bolted upright in my chair. Josie jumped and spilled her iced tea.

"Don't do that," she snapped, reaching for a napkin.

"Sorry," I said, helping her clean up the mess. "When I challenged Detective Renfro about the police not shutting down the cockfighting, he said that they had their reasons." I paused, then smiled at Gerald. "Then that proves there must be a connection between the cockfighting and the drug smuggling. The cops weren't shutting it down because they were in the middle of some sort of undercover investigation. That's it, isn't it?"

"You're good. Yeah, that's part of it," he said. "And when Detective Renfro saw you there last night, he was worried you might blow his cover."

"Detective Renfro was at the cockfight?" I said, surprised.

"He certainly was. And when he heard Rooster yell that it was a police raid, he freaked out. Now, he's worried that months of hard work could be going down the drain."

"I had no idea he was there," Josie said.

"He was the beer vendor," Gerald said.

"Really?" I said, impressed. "Great disguise." Then a thought popped, and I scowled. "He's the one who took the picture of us in the jeep, wasn't he?"

"He was," Gerald said, grinning. "He thought about paying you a visit, then decided to send the photo to the officers on patrol. Just to teach you a lesson."

"That little sneak," I said, frowning.

"Well, mission accomplished," Josie said. "I certainly learned a few things."

"Like not to listen to her hairbrained ideas?" Gerald said with a big grin.

126

"No, I always to listen to them for the entertainment value," Josie said. "I'm just rethinking the whole playing along part."

"So, all that stuff about us going to jail or being deported was just a bluff?" I said, ignoring both of them.

"No, not at all. There were some serious discussions about both of those possibilities," Gerald said. "But Detective Renfro and I eventually managed to calm the right people down. By the way, they're going to drop all the charges, but you need to make a generous donation to the Police Youth League."

"How many zeroes do you need on the check?"

"Four should do the trick," he said.

"Okay," I said, then refocused on the burning question. "So, somebody who was at that cockfight is smuggling dope?"

"It appears that way," Gerald said.

"But not William?"

"That's one of the problems," Gerald said. "In the past, William was involved in that particular activity. And his father had to pull every string and burn a lot of his political capital to make the problem go away after he got caught. But the Premier's reputation took a serious hit, and he almost lost his last election. If it turns out that William is still involved, he won't survive a second scandal."

"Again, why can't William just talk to his father about it?" Josie said.

"Because after the first incident, they stopped speaking," Gerald said. "His father basically disowned him. William has

127

been doing everything he can to get back in his father's good graces, but he's convinced that a second incident would make their falling-out permanent."

"Detective Renfro thinks that William could be the one he's looking for, right?" I said.

"The thought has crossed his mind, but he really doesn't have any proof," Gerald said. "But given his track record, you can see why Detective Renfro might think that. But even though he swears he's innocent, William isn't comfortable going to the police."

"I'd be going to the police," Josie said. "Assuming I was innocent."

"William doesn't trust the police," Gerald said, shrugging. "And after his last experience with them, I can't say that I really blame him."

"Oh, I don't know," I said, frowning. "I thought Officer Jones was an absolute delight to deal with."

"Suzy, you bit the guy," Gerald said. "What do you expect?"

"He's lucky that's all I did," I said. "William can't go to his dad, and he can't go to the police. So, he came to you?"

"He did," Gerald said. "William trusts me."

"And now you're coming to us," I said, beaming at him. "Because you trust *us*."

"Actually, I'm coming to you because I'm out of options," Gerald said with a shrug. "But we need to keep this strictly confidential."

"You told Detective Renfro you were going to ask us for help?" I said, raising an eyebrow at him.

"I did."

"Because you want someone around to make sure I stay safe."

"Your personal safety is certainly a major concern," Gerald said, nodding.

"And neither one of you would put me in the middle of an undercover operation unless you were pretty sure you could keep a close eye on what I was doing. I imagine Detective Renfro expects me to keep him in the loop."

"After he finally agreed to your involvement, that was the first thing that came out of his mouth. Actually, the term he used was *joined at the hip*."

"I take it Detective Renfro isn't thrilled with your plan," I said.

"He hates the idea," Gerald said.

"Then why did he agree?" Josie said, listening closely to the conversation.

"Good question," I said.

"Thanks. I thought so, too."

"Your little stunt last night put a serious crimp in his undercover operation since the police were forced to shut the cockfighting down. Now, Detective Renfro needs to regroup, and he finally agreed with me that you might be able to have a few conversations he can't."

I smiled at him and shook my head.

"Nice try, Gerald," I said, laughing. "Please, don't start blowing smoke up my skirt. Just tell me the real reason he finally agreed."

"Well," Gerald said, choosing his words carefully. "Detective Renfro isn't without political aspirations of his own. And I did happen to mention that I would appreciate his cooperation and be more than happy to push some of the requisite buttons on his behalf at the appropriate time."

"English, please, Gerald," I said, frowning.

"His career goal is to become the Police Commissioner," Gerald said.

"Is that a possibility?" Josie said.

"Sure," Gerald said, nodding. "He's a bit young, but Detective Renfro has an excellent reputation, and with the right recommendations, he would be in a good position should the job become vacant."

"Should or when?" I said, staring across the table at him.

"Oh, you caught that?" Gerald said as he reached for a piece of cheese.

"Are you saying that the Police Commissioner might somehow be involved in whatever is going on?"

"Gee, I sure hope not," he said, refilling everyone's iced tea. "But he is on shaky ground at the moment with the Premier."

"Because of this stuff?" I said, frowning.

"No, definitely not," Gerald said. "I doubt if the Premier or the Commissioner know the specifics of Detective Renfro's investigation."

"How is that even possible?" Josie said.

"They're both very busy people," Gerald said, deflecting the question with a shrug.

"I smell smoke," I said, laughing. "They don't know much about the investigation because Detective Renfro thinks one or both of them might be involved. That's it, isn't it, Gerald?"

"Perhaps," he said, staring out at the ocean.

"You dirty dog. You're next in line to be Premier, aren't you?" I said, staring at him.

"Suzy, I serve at the pleasure of my constituents," he said, going for solemn but unable to control his grin. "But if called upon, I would be honored to serve."

"You've got this whole thing figured out already, don't you?" I said.

"Only the possible scenarios," he said, shrugging. "It's not that hard. There are only a couple of ways this could play out."

"Yeah, I get it. If the Premier is involved in something nefarious, and you and Detective Renfro are instrumental in uncovering it, you slide right into his chair before it even has a chance to get cold. And bring Detective Renfro along with you.

But if the Premier isn't involved, and you're able to prove that, you'll have his eternal gratitude as well as probably become a national hero for defending the honor and integrity of the government. Either way, you come out of it smelling like a rose."

"You really are too smart for your own good," Gerald said, laughing.

"And you want to use me as what, some sort of bait?"

"Of course not," he said, glaring at me. "I want you to help William."

"And give yourself some additional cover if this blows up in your face?" I said. "You know, blame the crazy lady who spends her free time kidnapping roosters."

"I would never do anything like that, Suzy," he said, catching and holding my eyes with his until I finally nodded.

"Okay, I'll play," I said.

"Like you needed convincing," Chef Claire said, shaking her head.

"Oh, no, Gerald," Josie said. "Not the briar patch."

"You two can stop now," I said, glancing back and forth at them.

"No one can know I've asked you to help me out."

"Because you're worried about how the Premier and the Police Commissioner might react, right?"

"No, because your mother would kill me if she knew."

"Sure, sure," I said, nodding. Then another thought popped. "Hang on a sec. You said a few minutes ago that the connection between the cockfighting and smuggling was only part of the problem. There's more?"

"Yes," Gerald said, removing a folded piece of paper from his pocket. "There's this."

He handed it to me, and I carefully opened it. A message created from block letters was glued in a jumbled mess on the page.

"We know what you did," I said, reading aloud from the note. I glanced across the table at Gerald and waited.

"William found that in his office mail the day after Jensen's yacht blew up," Gerald said. "There wasn't any postmark on it."

"He's being blackmailed?"

"No, that's the strange thing," Gerald said. "William thinks somebody is trying to frame him for the Jensen's murders."

"They're not asking for any money?" I said.

"Not yet," he said. "And William doesn't think they're going to. He thinks that someone wants him arrested and put in jail."

"Because of what it could do to his father, right?" I said.

"You're on fire today," Gerald said, grinning.

"And on only three hours of sleep," Josie said, laughing.

"Aren't you sweet," I said, glancing over at her. "But I sure could use a nap." I turned to Gerald. "Is there anything else?"

"Just this," he said as he removed a second note from his pocket. "This was in his office mail yesterday. No postmark on this one either."

"Resignation is always an honorable option," I said, reading the message comprised of different sized letters glued onto the page. "It looks like somebody wants the Premier to ride off into the sunset."

"That can't be anything new," Josie said. "There's always a ton of people who want the person in power to go away."

"Of course," Gerald said. "But you usually don't see notes that look like that."

"Weird," I said, nodding. "So, somebody is trying to get to the Premier through his estranged son." I thought about it for a moment, but nothing specific popped to the surface. "You mentioned that both of the notes just happened to show up in his office mail."

"They did," Gerald said.

"What does William do for work?" I said casually as I poked my shoulder with a finger to test for sunburn.

"He owns a company that does a lot of work for construction companies," Gerald said, giving me a strange look.

"Construction?" I said, letting the idea roll around in my head. Then I frowned. "It wouldn't by any chance be a demolition company, would it?"

"Yes, as a matter of fact, it is," Gerald whispered.

"William's an explosives expert, isn't he?" I said.

"He is."

"Wow," Chef Claire said, shaking her head. "How does she put stuff together like that?"

"I have no idea," Josie said. "No wonder she gets along so well with the poodle."

"Let me guess," I said, ignoring them as I let my train of thought run wild. "There's a bunch of explosives that's gone missing from his company."

"Yes," Gerald said.

"Enough to blow up a yacht, right?"

"More than enough," he said, nodding. "I knew you were the right person to talk to."

"Don't you dare tell my mother," I said, holding my hand out.

"I wouldn't think of it," he said, accepting my pinkie swear.

Chapter 17

I waved as I strolled down the dock, untied the bow and stern lines, then tossed them onto the boat and hopped in.

"It looks like you've done this before," Detective Renfro said, apparently impressed.

"Boats?" I said. "Yeah, I've been on the water a few times." I glanced around at the boat I guessed was about twenty feet long and powered by a two hundred horsepower outboard motor. "This is nice. Works for fishing, skiing, or just tooling around, right?"

"Thanks, I like it," Detective Renfro said. "I bought it used a couple of years ago. I finally decided it didn't make any sense living here if I didn't have a boat."

"Can't argue with that," I said. "But was it really necessary for us to go out on the water?"

"I don't think it's a good idea for us to be seen together," he said, firing up the engine and accelerating away from the dock.

The boat planed and I let the sun wash over me as we headed for deep water. A couple miles from shore, Detective Renfro slowed to an idle then turned the engine off. We began a slow drift as the breeze caught the boat and started to do its thing. The detective grabbed two beers from the cooler and handed me one.

"Leftover inventory from your moonlighting as a beer vendor?" I said, holding up my can.

"Yeah," he said, taking a long sip. "I couldn't believe it when I saw you guys there."

"I can't believe you took that photo then sold us out to the cops."

"Sorry, but I couldn't resist," he said, laughing.

"Well played, Detective," I said, raising my beer in salute.

I took a sip and stretched out on the seat that ran along the starboard side.

"Good call coming out here. It's a gorgeous day," I said, nodding as I gazed out at the open water. "This isn't far from where the yacht blew up, is it?"

"No, it's pretty close," he said, stretching out on the seat across from me.

"Where you ever able to recover anything after the explosion?" I said.

"Nothing much of any real use," he said. "We found Jensen's hat floating on the surface. And we also found a set of keys attached to one of those bobbers. We think they belonged to his wife. The rest of what was left is now resting comfortably somewhere on the bottom of the ocean."

"The water is deep around here," I said, glancing over the side of the boat.

"It is," he said, taking another sip. "There's no way we'll ever recover any of it. Not that anybody has any interest in looking for it."

I nodded then yawned.

"Am I boring you already?" he said, laughing.

"No, not at all. I'm still a little behind in my sleep."

"Stop spending late nights at the police station."

"Yeah, thanks for the tip," I said, making a face at him. "Okay, I guess we should get started. I assume you want to go over the ground rules first?"

"That's as good a place as any to start," he said, sitting up. "We need to agree that you'll give me advance notice of everyone you plan to talk to. As well as where and when."

"I can live with that," I said.

"And I'll expect a full report on each conversation," he said.

"Of course," I said, stifling another yawn. "Do you have a list of people you'd like me to talk to?"

"I do," he said, reaching for his notepad.

"The Premier's son?"

"Yeah, but not right away," Detective Renfro said. "I'd like to know a bit more before you talk to him. How would you approach William?"

"I thought I'd play up his connection to Gerald. Maybe William will open up to me after he knows that I've talked with Gerald about his problem."

"Out of a concern for his well-being," the detective said, nodding. "Yeah, I like that."

"You really think he might be involved in smuggling?"

"Given his past, I do," he said, draining the last of his beer. "Wow, that went down way too easy."

"I don't like him for it," I said, shaking my head.

"Really? Do tell," he said, hopping up to grab two more beers from the cooler.

"Those notes he received about how they knew he blew up the yacht. It just seems too easy. And Gerald said the kid has been doing everything he could to get back in his father's good graces."

"Maybe he thought his father would give him a medal for blowing up Jensen's yacht," he said, handing me a fresh beer.

"The Premier and Jensen had history?" I said, finishing my first beer.

"They did. And it was based on mutual hatred. Jensen did everything he could to undermine the Premier every chance he got," Detective Renfro said, stretching back out on the seat.

"Why would he do that?"

"Well, the Premier has tried to crack down on a lot of the money laundering that goes on in the islands, and he's been tough on crime. If you were smuggling drugs and dealing with a lot of cash, that seems like a couple of good reasons."

"Did Jensen pump money into his opponent's campaigns?"

"He did. As well as try to get several local reporters on his payroll to do his bidding," the detective said, then paused for effect. "And possibly a few cops as well."

"He bought off some of the local cops?" I said, sitting up.

"You hear stories," the detective said, shrugging.

"Interesting," I said, debating about whether or not to broach the subject. Then I decided I might as well toss a line in the water. "Do you think the Police Commissioner might be corrupt?"

The detective remained silent for several seconds, then shrugged again.

"You hear stories."

"Gerald said the Commissioner and the Premier aren't on good terms at the moment," I said, taking a sip of my fresh beer.

"They never have been," he said. "Our Premier is very focused on change. The Commissioner is more interested in, let's call it, preserving the status quo. You know, maintaining the tradition."

"A tradition of corruptness?"

"You said it, not me."

"Was the Commissioner close to Jensen?"

"I believe he was at one point."

"You said you weren't aware that Jensen was smuggling dope, right?"

"Until his yacht blew up, I didn't have a clue," Detective Renfro said. "Then a few things started making some more sense."

"And got you thinking that the Commissioner might somehow be involved?"

"Yeah," he said, deep in thought. "But I can't figure out how he, Jensen, and William might have been connected."

I gave it some thought, then let it go. I was going to need a whole bunch more information before I could make that leap.

"When in doubt, poke the bear," I said, staring out at the water.

"That's why you're here," he said, laughing.

"I'd like to have a chat with the Commissioner," I said.

"How are you going to do that without making him suspicious?"

"I'm about to give him some money."

"Oh, the donation," Detective Renfro said after thinking it through. "I like it. But don't try to get cute with him."

"I can't help being cute, Detective," I said, laughing as I struck a pose for him.

"You know what I mean."

"Yeah, I got it. In addition to talking to William, you want me to talk with Jennifer Jensen again and the people staying at her house, right?"

"I do," he said, nodding.

"You practicing, Detective?" I said, grinning at him. "I suggest you put a little bass in your voice."

"What on earth are you talking about?"

"You said *I do*. I thought you might be practicing for your upcoming nuptials."

"I'm sure I'll be able to manage," he said, shaking his head. "You are so weird."

"Yeah, I really need to start working on that."

"You think you'll be able to come up with a plausible reason to drop by the daughter's house?"

"I'll have to give it some thought," I said. "But I'm sure I'll be able to figure out a way to use the dog as an excuse."

"Good," he said, nodding.

"Is that all the folks you want me to have a chat with?"

"Just about."

"There's more?" I said, frowning.

"Just one."

I let my mind wander through the possibilities, came up empty, then a thought popped into my head.

"Please tell me you're not thinking about the guy who ran the cockfight?" I said, scowling at the memory.

"Yeah, Ramon," Detective Renfro said. "That's the one. Well done. I never thought you'd get it."

"Yuk," I said. "The man's a pig."

"He certainly is. But we're stuck at the moment when it comes to Ramon."

"You think he might be the one who's moving the coke once it hits land?" I said.

"Based on some of the people I've seen him talking with at recent cockfights, I think it's a possibility."

"Some of those people were the ones staying at Jennifer Jensen's place, right?"

"Well done," he said. "I'm impressed."

"I have my moments," I said. "What does Ramon do for work when he's not putting on cockfights?"

"He works construction," Detective Renfro said, then let his comment hang in the air.

"On demolition crews?" I said, cocking my head at him.

"Occasionally."

"He works for William?"

"Occasionally."

I stared down at my rapidly disappearing second beer then set it down next to me.

"I'm getting a headache," I said, reaching into my bag for a bottle of Advil.

"Seasick?"

"Neuron overload," I said, washing four pills down with a small sip of beer. "This is a lot to process."

"Take your time," he said, laughing. "I've been working on it for months. Let's have some lunch. Maybe that will help your headache."

"It's certainly worth a shot," I said, following him to the cooler. He handed me a thick sandwich, and I unwrapped it and took a bite. I nodded my approval then took a bigger bite. "Have you guys set a wedding date?"

"We're getting close," he said. "I can't wait. We're hoping to have to have our first kid right away."

"Me too," I blurted, then shook my head and frowned.

"What's the matter?"

"Wow. That's the first time I've ever said that out loud."

"How did it feel?" he said.

"Not bad. Not bad at all," I said, smiling. "But do me a favor."

"What's that?"

"Don't tell my mother."

"Okay, but why don't you want her to know?"

"I'd like to get her through the wedding first."

"Sure, I get that. Because it would be more than she can handle at one time, right?"

"You really haven't been paying attention have you, Detective?"

Chapter 18

My strategy to get a meeting with the Police Commissioner had been easy to formulate and was based on the idea that there were very few public officials who didn't like to see their picture in the paper, assuming that the photo was flattering and didn't display the official in a comprising position or caught doing something nefarious. And since I would merely be handing over a check to the Commissioner, I thought my thinking was solid. My theory was confirmed when I got a call from someone on the Commissioner's staff inviting me to a presentation ceremony in Georgetown.

I parked across the street from a soccer field that definitely needed an upgrade. And if that was how the Commissioner was planning on spending the ten grand I was giving him, it was money well spent. A small bandstand sat in the corner of the field that was closest to the street, and I saw a couple dozen people sitting in folding chairs in front of the makeshift stage along with several kids in various soccer uniforms in a circle casually kicking a ball back and forth. I approached the bandstand unsure where to go and looked around. I saw Detective Renfro sitting in one of the folding chairs, but when our eyes met, he gave me a slight shake of his head, and I decided to keep my distance.

"You must be Ms. Chandler," a uniformed policewoman said with a smile and an extended hand.

"I am," I said, returning her handshake. "Please, call me Suzy."

"Suzy, it is," she said. "I'm Officer Fritz."

"Please tell me your first name isn't On The," I said.

"Oh, good one," she deadpanned. "Never heard that one before."

"Sorry. I couldn't resist. Where do you want me to sit?" I said, glancing around.

"Up there," she said, pointing at the bandstand. "We'll go up as soon as the Commissioner arrives."

"Okay," I said, rocking back and forth on my heels as I watched the kids continue to kick the ball around.

"Barb, he just called and is on his way," a cop in uniform said as he approached his colleague. Then he saw me. "Ms. Chandler."

"Officer Jones," I said, surprised to see him. Then I caught a glimpse of the bandage on his hand. I did my best to hide my smile. "Wounded in the line of duty?"

"Yeah, I got bit by a wild animal the other night," he said, glaring at me. "The doctor says I'll be fine. But I did get a rabies shot just in case."

"Maybe you'll get a commendation for bravery," I said, then muttered under my breath. "Ya big baby."

146

"Okay, guys," Officer Fritz said, scolding us. "Don't start. Today is for the kids."

"Then Ms. Chandler should feel right at home," Officer Jones said before he walked away and took a seat in front of the bandstand.

"Don't mind him," Officer Fritz said. "He's been taking a lot of ribbing since your incident."

"Because he allowed himself to get bit by a girl?" I said.

"Yeah," she said, laughing. "That's pretty much it. Oh, good. He's here."

I turned and watched a large balding man with grey around the temples briskly walk toward us. Two other uniformed officers nipped at his heels as they tried to keep up with the Commissioner's pace. He came to a stop right in front of me and gave me a thorough once-over. Then he nodded and extended his hand.

"It's nice to finally meet you, Ms. Chandler," he said. "You look much better in person than your mug shot."

"Thanks, I'm glad to hear that," I said, wincing from the strong grip.

He gave me a small grin as he squeezed my hand, and I was sure he'd given me the handshake of death just to make a point about who was in charge.

Like I'd want his job.

"Okay, I'm here," he said, turning to Officer Fritz. "Let's do this."

"We're just waiting for Jerome. He's running a bit late," she said, then turned to me. "Jerome is the president of the Youth League."

"And a devotee of island time," the Commissioner said. "Jerome is going to be late for his own funeral. Come. Let's go sit on the bandstand and get out of this sun."

I followed him up a small set of steps and stood quietly off to one side as he surveyed the crowd and waved to several people. Then he gestured at a chair and sat down next to me. I had hoped for a few minutes alone with him, and it looked like this was going to be my best shot. But before I could get my opening question out, he beat me to the punch.

"Been to any good cockfights lately?" he said, glancing over at me.

"Yeah, I guess I should apologize for my behavior, Commissioner," I said. "I just take animal cruelty very seriously."

"Understandable," he said, nodding. "But in the future, how about you try to remember that you're a guest in our country?"

"Absolutely," I said, then had to ask. "How close was I to getting deported?"

The Commissioner extended a hand and held his thumb and index finger about a quarter inch apart in front of my face.

"That close, huh?"

"Indeed," he said. "You're lucky that Gerald has as much juice as he does. If it had been up to me, I would have put you in a leaky boat and wished you good luck finding land," he said with an evil grin.

"Okay, now we understand each other," I said, annoyed. "I take it you're a fan of cockfights."

The Commissioner slowly turned his head and gave me an angry stare. It made the hairs on the back of my neck stand up, but I held my ground.

"You need to be very careful, Ms. Chandler."

"Is that a threat, Commissioner? Or just a piece of friendly advice?"

"Take it any way you want," he said, shrugging. "But thanks for the check. Ten thousand was very generous."

"It was the least I could do," I said, staring out at the small crowd.

"No, actually, five thousand was the least you could do," he said, laughing.

"I was prepared to give you twenty," I said, beaming at him.

"I'll keep that in mind the next time you do something incredibly stupid," the Commissioner said, waving at someone sitting in the front row.

"All I did was save some defenseless roosters."

"And nearly caused a public riot in the process."

"Tomato, tomahto."

"Not to mention the damage you did to a very important investigation," he muttered under his breath.

"Really? An investigation. Do tell," I said, grinning at him.

"Not a chance in hell," he said, not returning the smile.

"What sort of investigation do you need to do with illegal cockfighting?" I said, going for demure. "It seems like a very straightforward activity. Barbaric, but straightforward."

"Yes, one would think," he said, nodding again as he glanced out at the crowd that looked like it was going to remain sparse.

"Of course, an activity like that must attract all sort of shady characters," I said. "You know, evildoers."

"Evildoers?" he said, laughing as he looked over at me. "That's a Batman reference, right?"

"I'm not sure," I said, shrugging. "I'm not a big fan of the superhero genre. Those movies are way too loud and violent. You know, all those explosions and things blowing up."

I let my comment hang in the air and waited for his reaction. But all I got from him were narrowed eyes and a slight change in his posture. I guess you don't make it all the way to top cop by revealing too much to strangers.

"Gerald warned me about you," he said after a long pause.

"And?"

"And he was right," the Commissioner said, then stood up and stared at a man who was making double-time toward the bandstand. "He's finally here. It's about time."

The man climbed the short set of steps carrying an oversized cardboard check. He leaned it against the podium then wiped his hands on his pants and extended his hand to me.

"Sorry I'm late, Commissioner," he said, shaking my hand. "It took them forever to deliver the check. You must be Ms. Chandler. I'm Jerome Albert, President of the Police Youth League."

"It's nice to meet you, Jerome," I said.

"Thank you so much for your generous donation," Jerome said.

"No problem. It was almost the least I could do," I said, flashing the unamused Commissioner a grin.

"Okay," Jerome said, confused. "Why don't we get started before all our guests fry in this heat?"

He briefly ran through the process with us then approached the podium. He welcomed everyone, introduced the Commissioner and me to polite applause, then turned the microphone over to the Commissioner who managed to thank me without choking on his words. The Commissioner explained to the crowd that the funds would be used to renovate the soccer field, then he motioned for Jerome and me to stand next to him as we posed for pictures. The Commissioner stood in the center of the photo and held the poster check up with one hand.

"I'm going to put my arm around your waist for the picture," he said.

"Okay," I said with a casual shrug. "Knock yourself out."

"Try not to bite me."

Chapter 19

We grabbed a handful of tennis balls and headed across the lawn with five excited dogs leading the way to the gate that led down to the beach. All three of us removed our sandals when we reached the soft sand, and we each fired a couple of the balls in different directions and laughed as we watched the dogs try to make up their minds about which one they wanted to go after. Soon, they all decided, and we had a few minutes of peace and quiet as we strolled toward the edge of the water.

Captain was the first dog to return carrying three balls in his mouth. He dropped them at Josie's feet and stared expectantly out at the water.

"No," she said, shaking her head. "You've been in the water enough for one day."

Captain woofed his displeasure but raced off in pursuit when Josie threw one of the balls downwind along the beach. We repeated the process with all five dogs as we walked through the sand toward my mother's place.

"You ready for this?" Chef Claire said.

"Sure, she can't still be mad at me, right?" I said, then looked at her. "Can she?"

"She was in a pretty good mood at lunch today," Chef Claire said.

"That's good to hear," I said.

"Of course, you weren't there."

Josie snorted then threw a couple of tennis balls onto the path that led up to my mother's backyard. All five dogs chased the balls then just kept going and disappeared from view. We followed them up the path, and they were already saying hello to everyone by the time we arrived. Then the dogs started roughhousing on the lawn. I glanced around and noticed the table was set for eight. I did the math, came up one short, then decided that the eighth person had to be Gerald. Henry was working the grill and Josie and Chef Claire wandered over to see what was on the menu. I saw Rooster and Paulie sitting poolside and headed for them.

"Well, look who finally worked up the courage to show her face," Rooster said, laughing.

"Don't start," I said, giving both of them a hug before sitting down. "But I figured I've waited long enough. How's she doing?"

"She's good," Paulie said. "Just don't bring up the other night and you'll be fine."

My mother and Gerald came out of the house carrying bowls and set them down on the table. Deciding I couldn't avoid it any longer, I got up and crossed the lawn. My mother watched me closely as I approached, then nodded.

"Good evening, darling."

153

"Hi, Mom," I said, giving her a long hug. "It's nice to see you. And, again, I want to apologize."

"Apologize? What for?" she said, raising an eyebrow.

"For being late to dinner," I said. "What else?"

She laughed and pulled me in for another hug.

"What am I going to with you?"

"It's a question for the ages, Mom."

"Indeed. I need to head back inside for a bit."

"You need a hand?" I said.

"No, I'm fine," she said. "Just sit here and keep Gerald company."

We watched her stroll back toward the house, then we sat down at the table. Gerald grabbed a bottle of wine and poured. We clinked glasses then settled into our chairs and got comfortable.

"Well, that certainly went better than I expected," I said after my mother disappeared into the house.

"She's fine," Gerald said, waving it off. "Has she ever been that mad at you before?"

"Is there much sand at the beach?" I said.

"Got it," Gerald said. "How did the presentation ceremony go today?"

"It was pretty uneventful," I said. "But the Commissioner doesn't like me."

"I wouldn't worry about it," he said, taking a sip of wine. "The Commissioner doesn't seem to like anybody."

"He said that, if it hadn't been for you, I would have been deported in a leaky boat."

"Ah, don't mention it," Gerald said. "Besides, the place wouldn't be the same without you. What's your take on him?"

"He's definitely all cop. At least, that's the impression he likes to give. And I know that what I did was pretty stupid, but he seemed way too angry."

"How so?"

"It was like I'd somehow touched a nerve. It was strange."

"Do you think he might be involved?" Gerald said, swirling the wine in his glass.

"Maybe. I did get a bit of a reaction out of him when I dropped a comment about things blowing up."

"Oh, Suzy," he said, frowning. "Please, tell me you didn't do that."

"It's okay," I said. "I worked it into a conversation about superheroes."

Gerald stared at me, bewildered.

"Relax, Gerald. Did you talk to Detective Renfro today?"

"I did," he said, topping off our wine. "He's personally started doing some surveillance on the guy who was putting on the cockfights."

"Ramon."

"That's the one. But he hasn't seen anything suspicious yet. Ramon goes to work in the morning, stops by some hole-in-the-wall bar after work, then heads home."

155

"Does he live in the house in front of the place where the cockfight was held?"

"He does. By himself."

"Geez, I'm surprised," I said. "I thought a charming guy like that would have to beat the women off with a stick."

"Or an armed rooster," Gerald said.

"Funny," I said, raising my glass in salute. "I'm heading back to Jennifer's place in the morning. Should I send her your best?"

"No, don't do that," he said, shaking his head. "Have you figured out what sort of excuse you're going to use for dropping in unannounced."

"I'm still working on that."

Seemingly on cue, Polly got to her feet, picked up a nearby tennis ball, then trotted toward me. She sat down at my feet and dropped the tennis ball. She stared back and forth at me and the ball. Then she trotted off and returned with a second ball. Eventually, a half dozen tennis balls were scattered around my chair. I finally got the point and laughed.

"What a great idea," I said, rubbing the poodle's head. "I think that just might work."

"You're speaking dog now?" Gerald said, staring at the poodle.

"Well, it's not like I'm fluent."

Chapter 20

I made the drive to Jennifer Jensen's place from memory and parked in front. I considered knocking on the front door, but I again heard splashing and laughter coming from the pool area. I wandered along the path next to the house that led to the backyard and had a déjà vu moment. The same couple was stretched out next to each other in the same lounge chair smoking weed and making short work of a cooler filled with Caybrew. This I knew because of the empty beer cans circling them on the tile. The other three people were in the shallow end in pretty much the same spot they'd been when I last visited. But they seemed to have added a twist by playing a game that involved seeing who could hold their breath underwater the longest, then the losers would have to do a shot of what looked like tequila. It seemed to be a good way to spend the day as long as your goal was to ensure that at least one of your fellow pool mates drowned before lunch. Regardless, all three were oblivious to my presence so I headed for the couple in the lounge chair and soon decided I would have to talk fast since they were both well into what Josie liked to call the Double-Baked Zone; baked on the outside by the sun, baked internally by the behavior modifying substance of choice. Or in this case, substances.

"Hey, look who's here," the man said, glancing up at me behind his sunglasses. "What's your name again?"

"Suzy," I said, sitting down on the edge of the recliner next to them. "I don't think I got your names the other day."

"I'm Danny," he said, offering me a beer I waved off. "And this is Terry."

"Danny and Terry," I said, smiling back and forth at them as I committed their names to memory. "Another day in paradise, huh?"

"Yeah, it's a tough life," the woman named Terry said, then giggled. "You want to get high?"

"No, thanks," I said, holding my hands up. "But you guys go right ahead. I'm sitting upwind."

For some reason, they both laughed long and hard. While I waited for them to find their focus, I watched the game in progress in the pool. Two men surfaced within seconds of each other and stood in the shallow end gasping for breath Moments later, a woman popped to the surface, then placed her elbows on the edge of the pool and laughingly poured two large shots and handed them to her vanquished competitors.

"What's the name of that game they're playing?" I said, intrigued by their strange behavior.

"Arrack Attack," she said.

"I beg your pardon?" I said, frowning.

"Arrack Attack," she repeated. "Arrack is a liquor that's made in lots of places in Asia. But we like the one that comes out of Sri Lanka."

"Sri Lanka?" I said, thoroughly confused, then remembered who I was talking to. "Sure, now I get it. You buy fabric and clothing there, right?"

"Yeah, primarily silk and batik," she said as she fired up a joint the size of a taquito. She took several quick puffs to get it lit, then inhaled deeply and passed it to Danny who needed more about as much I needed to see the menu at C's before ordering. "They have some really cool stuff, and the markups are *a-ma-zing*."

"Sure, sure," I said, glancing at Danny who looked like he was about to try and talk with a lungful of smoke. This should be good, I decided, and I smiled at him while I waited.

"And it's…a great place…to party," he said, then exhaled loudly. "Whew," he said, exhausted from the effort. "You want to try the Arrack? Maybe join the game in the pool?"

"No, I'm good thanks," I said. "I don't even like to get my hair wet in the shower."

Danny frowned at me then shrugged and took another hit before passing it back to his lounge chair partner.

"I've never been to Sri Lanka. But I hear it's nice. Do you spend a lot of time there?"

"We do," Terry said. "At least we did. Now, I'm sure what we're going to do."

"Because of what might happen with the Jensen's company?" I said.

"Yeah, there's that," she said. "Not to mention their private island."

"They had a private island in Sri Lanka?" I said, leaning forward.

"Yeah, it's amazing," Danny said, his eyes half-closed. "We used to go there for company meetings a couple of times a year."

"Has Jennifer made any decisions about what she's going to do?" I said.

"If she has, she hasn't shared them with us," Danny said, shrugging. "But that's the way the Pink Princess operates."

Terry snorted smoke and giggled.

"That's Danny's new nickname for her," Terry said, taking another hit to reload her lungs. "Before she dyed her hair, she was the Green Gofer."

I forced myself to remain silent as the pair of insensitive and ungrateful, sorry excuse for houseguests again chortled.

"If Jennifer decides to run the company herself, will you be sticking around?" I said when they recovered.

"No way," Danny said. "We're out regardless of what she decides to do. We've been talking about setting up our own company for a long time. This seems like the right time to do it. In fact, we've got several-"

"Oh, let's not talk shop, Danny," Terry said, squeezing his hand as she gave him a warning look I couldn't miss. "That's just going to bore, Suzy."

"No, it's okay," I said with a smile. "I'd love to hear about your plans."

"Maybe some other time," Danny said, chagrined and massaging his hand. "Besides, we really haven't worked out a lot of the details yet."

I imagine that polishing off a couple of blunts before noon, washed down with a twelve-pack, could definitely put a crimp in one's ability to develop a coherent business plan. And since it looked like they weren't long for the conscious world, I shifted gears.

"Do the folks in the pool work with you?"

They both glanced at the three in the shallow end who appeared to be taking a break and trying to catch their breath.

"They all work for the company," Terry said. "But they handle security."

"Security?" I said, frowning.

"Yeah, you know," Danny said. "Making sure the employees and company property stay safe."

"The owner and his yacht just blew up," I said, frowning at them.

"Yeah," Danny said, shrugging at me with a blank stare. "I guess they sort of whiffed on that one."

"Ya think?" I said, baffled. "So, I imagine the three of them will be looking for other jobs?"

"Eventually," Terry said.

"Probably as soon as they get through the last couple of cases of Arrack," he said.

He and Terry burst out laughing again. Then he relit the joint, took a hit and passed it to her. I officially hit the wall and stood up.

"Is Jennifer inside?"

"That would be my guess," Terry said. "She's been keeping to herself since the accident."

"Thanks," I said, sliding my hands into the pockets of my shorts. "Nice seeing you guys."

"Yeah, it was," Danny said. "Stop by the next time you feel like partying."

"I'll do that," I said, then a question surfaced. "Hey, I've been looking for things to do at night around here. You guys got any suggestions?"

"You mean, apart from drinking and eating?" Terry said.

"Yeah, I've got those pretty well covered," I said, nodding. "I was talking about doing something a bit out of the ordinary."

"Well, we thought we found one the other night," Danny said. "But that turned out to be a major disappointment."

"What was that?" I said, going for casual.

"We went to a cockfight," he said. "But the cops raided the place before it could even get started."

162

"People freaked out," Terry said. "I almost got trampled trying to get out of there."

"Yeah, sorry about that," I whispered.

"What?"

"Nothing," I said, shaking my head. "A cockfight, huh?"

"Yeah, but it was nothing compared to the ones we've been to in Asia," Danny said.

"Oh, you're a fan?" I said, giving him my best crocodile smile.

"Love it," he said, nodding. "There's just something about watching animals fight to the death."

"You don't think it's a bit barbaric?"

"Nah, those birds are way too far down the food chain to worry about," he said, waving my question off.

"I see," I said, needing to leave before I forced him into my own version of Arrack Attack in the deep end of the pool. "Well, good luck with the new company. Given what you've told me, I'm sure you'll do very well."

"Gee, thanks," he said, reaching into the cooler for two fresh beers.

I headed toward the house but not before I caught the cold stare Terry was giving me.

I knocked on the sliding glass doors, and soon Jennifer slid one of them open and stared at me. She was definitely surprised to see me and seemed preoccupied but not annoyed I'd shown up unannounced.

"Suzy," she said, stepping back and waving me inside. "Come on in."

"Hi, Jennifer," I said, stepping inside. I squinted until my eyes adjusted to the change in light then smiled at her. "How are you doing?"

"I've been better," she said with a small shrug. "Can I get you some coffee? I just made a pot."

"Sounds good, thanks."

I followed her into the kitchen and sat down on one of the stools next to the island. She handed me a mug then sat down across from me. I splashed a bit of milk in my cup then stirred and took a sip. I glanced around the well-appointed kitchen then noticed the curious look she was giving me.

"You're wondering why I'm here, right?"

"Maybe a little," she said, sipping her coffee.

"It's about Polly," I said.

"Is she okay?"

"She's fine," I said. "I was just wondering if you have any of her dog toys here."

"Why, did she ask you to come over and get them for her?" she said, laughing.

"What?"

"Family joke," Jennifer said, shaking her head. "That dog always seemed to be a step ahead of everybody."

"I have to say that she is a bit spooky to be around at times," I said, nodding. "I've never met a dog quite like her before."

"I'm surprised she didn't write you a list of the toys she wants back," Jennifer said, laughing again. Then she paused to look at me. "She didn't do that, right?"

"No," I said, laughing along. "But I think she was looking for pen and paper just before I left this morning."

"I guess we're lucky she doesn't have opposable thumbs," Jennifer said. "How did she tell you she wanted her toys?"

"Last night, we were sitting outside, and Polly dropped a tennis ball at my feet then kept looking back and forth at me and the ball. At first, I thought she wanted me to throw it, but then she trotted off and brought me another ball. She kept doing it until I eventually figured out what she was trying to tell me. I spend my entire life with dogs, but I have to admit that it kind of freaked me out."

"That's our girl, Polly," Jennifer said, sipping her coffee.

"So, do you have some of her toys here?"

"Oh, yeah," she said. "My father couldn't walk past a pet store without buying her at least one. Help yourself to them."

"Thanks," I said, glancing out the window at the pool area. "I see your house guests are still here."

"Yes, they certainly are. They're like a bad rash you can't rid of," she said, following my eyes. "Are they still playing that stupid drinking game?"

"Well, the three people who work security are," I said. "But despite their ability to hold their breath, I don't think it would be a good idea for Danny and Terry get in the water at the moment. They're pretty hammered."

"They're always hammered," she said, shrugging. "But I'm sure all of them will be leaving soon."

"To go back to work?"

"I seriously doubt that," she said. "As soon as they hear that I'm selling this place and my dad's company, I'm sure they'll be hitting the road."

"You decided to sell?" I said, giving her room to top off our mugs.

"I have," she said, sitting back down.

"I'm in the middle of selling a company at the moment, too."

"Really?" she said, cocking her head at me. "How do you feel about that?"

"It feels fantastic," I said, laughing.

"Yeah, me too," she said, raising her mug in salute before taking a sip.

"Have you decided what you're going to do next?"

"Well, my plans are a bit up in the air at the moment," she said, exhaling softly. "I didn't think they would be, but they are. Such is life, huh?"

"Yeah, I get that," I said. "Problem?"

"Yeah. A *love* problem."

"Oh, don't you just hate when that happens?"

"They're never fun. Especially when the problem is coming from outside the relationship."

"Do you want to talk about it?"

"Not really," she said, shaking her head.

"Fair enough. Can I ask you a question?"

"Now you need permission?" she said, laughing.

"Yeah, I really need to start working on that," I said, shrugging. "My question is about Gerald."

"Gerald? What about him?" she said, suddenly wary.

"He mentioned that the two of you used to be…an item," I said, choosing my words carefully.

"An item?" she said, grinning. "That doesn't sound like something Gerald would say. He's usually a bit more graphic."

"My term, not his."

"Yes, we were involved for a while," she said. "I really enjoyed spending time with him. And I probably would have continued seeing him."

"But you met somebody else, right?"

"As a matter of fact, I did," she said, nodding.

"And that person is the other party in your current love problem."

"How the heck did you know that?" she said, surprised.

"Lucky guess."

That was the truth. It was. But I could tell I was about to cross a line with her, so I let it go.

167

"What are you going to do with your parents' island in Sri Lanka?"

"Danny and Terry are chatty today, aren't they?" she said, shaking her head. "Why do you ask? You want to buy it?"

"No, thanks," I said. "I've already got more waterfront property than I know what to do with."

"That's a good problem to have," she said. "I'll be selling the island and some other properties just as soon as the lawyers are able to track down the deeds and ownership records."

"They can't find them?"

"They think they might have gotten destroyed in the explosion," she said. "They're currently working on some replacement documents."

"Do you know where you're going to move?"

"We've been talking about Europe," she said. "We'd like to see some different seasons for a change."

"Be careful what you wish for," I said, flashing back to our recent experience at home with an early and brutal winter. "Have the police been back recently?"

"No, I think they've moved on from their original theory that I was somehow involved," she said.

"Well, that's good news."

"One would think," she said, getting up from her chair. "Let me get those toys for you."

I waited in the kitchen until she returned carrying a cardboard box overflowing with dog toys of all shapes and sizes.

I thanked her, then headed outside where all five of the partygoers were sprawled out on lounge chairs sound asleep. I lumbered along the path that led back to my jeep and hoisted the box into the back seat. I climbed in and headed for home. A few minutes later, my phone rang, and I checked the number and slid it into its dashboard holder.

"Detective Renfro," I said. "You're timing is perfect."

"Why's that?" he said.

"I just came from Jennifer Jensen's place."

"And?"

"And she has decided to sell her father's company and the house here in Cayman. She's talking about moving to Europe as soon as she gets her *love problem* sorted out."

"Interesting," he said. "Who's she in love with, and why is she having problems?"

"She wouldn't say."

"You're losing your touch," he said, laughing.

"Oh, let's hope not," I said. "And I got some strange vibes from a couple of the people who work for the company. Did you meet the couple that handles the fabrics and clothing?"

"The Stoner Twins? Yeah, I met them. I can't wait to hear all about it. We'll take the boat out."

"I'm free at the moment," I said, glancing at my watch.

"No, I can't right now," he said.

"Because you're out fighting evildoers, right?" I said, laughing.

"No, because I'm on my way to arrest the Premier's son for the murder of Jack and Jill Jensen," he said without emotion.

"You're joking."

"About something like that? Never."

"Why are you arresting him now?"

"Do you remember when I mentioned that we were going to keep a patrol boat checking for debris around the area where the yacht blew up?"

"I do," I said, slowing down. "You said it was a million to one shot."

"I guess sometimes long shots do pay off," he said. "They found a couple of things floating on the surface."

"Things that fit with the prevailing direction of the current?"

"Yeah."

"What did they find?"

"Pieces of wood from a box that dynamite comes in," he said.

"Is that all?" I said, frowning.

"The name of William's company was stamped on the side of one of the pieces."

"Is that enough evidence to make an arrest with?"

"Probably not," he said. "Unless you also happened to find shards of fiberglass embedded into the wood. And some feathers and a few bloodstains."

I pulled the jeep over to the side of the road and rubbed my forehead as I felt the onset of a headache.

"Are you still there?" he said after a long pause.

"Yeah, I'm here," I said, exhaling loudly. "Wow. That's pretty incriminating evidence."

"That's what we thought. Hence, our decision to arrest him."

"Would it be possible for me to talk to him?" I said.

"Not until he makes bail, it won't."

"Will the judge grant bail?"

"Suzy, the kid's the Premier's son," Detective Renfro said. "What do you think?"

"There's no need to get snarky, Detective," I snapped. "Geez, I was convinced William wasn't involved."

"You need to start trusting my instincts," he said.

"Yeah, thanks for the tip," I said, my mind racing. "Can we take your boat out tomorrow?"

"I think I can make that work," he said. "Today's is going to be a zoo as soon as the word gets out. This is going to be a major story."

"Just a word of caution to you and Gerald," I said, pulling back onto the road.

"What's that?"

"Try to avoid taking any victory laps."

"I'll do my best," he said, sounding way too happy.

"And whatever you do, don't start measuring your new offices for curtains just yet."

"Funny."

"I really wasn't going for funny, Detective."

Chapter 21

I stared at the reflected images in the mirror behind the glass shelves the bottles were sitting on, and my eyes landed on a bottle of Arrack. I leaned forward, shifting in my seat enough to get Josie's attention.

"Penny for your thoughts," she said, glancing up from her menu.

"That's about all they're worth tonight," I said, waving to Rocco who was standing on the other side of the bar reviewing a stack of receipts.

"You folks ready to order?"

"I am," Josie said, then proceeded to recite her order.

"Really?" Rocco said with a frown when she finally finished. "You expecting company?"

"I had an early lunch."

"New York medium rare, house salad, side of fried mushrooms?" he said to me.

"Perfect. Thanks, Rocco," I said, then pointed behind the bar. "Can I see that bottle of Arrack?"

He handed me the bottle, and I turned it over in my hands.

"Do we sell any of this stuff?" I said, setting the bottle down on the bar.

"Not a lot," he said, shaking his head. "But we had a group in the other night that killed a bottle."

"Two men and a woman? Looked a bit like cops?" I said.

"Yeah, that sounds like them," Rocco said. "How the heck did you know that?"

"Lucky guess."

"But there were four of them at the table."

"What did the other one look like?" I said.

"Big greasy bald guy who had enormous gold hoops dangling from his ears," he said, shaking his head. "Not a good look. I pegged him as a local."

"Ramon had dinner with them?" I said to Josie.

"Who's Ramon?" Rocco said.

"He's the guy who organized the cockfight," I said as several questions began bouncing around.

"The one the night you got arrested and bit the cop?"

"Yeah, that's the one," I said, making a face at him.

Josie, her interest piqued, picked up the bottle of Arrack and examined it.

"Sri Lanka?" she said, frowning. "I had him pegged as a beer with rum chaser kind of guy. What's Ramon doing drinking Sri Lankan liquor?"

"Trying to fit in, I imagine," I said, then glanced at Rocco. "Did they meet anybody else here?"

"Not that I noticed," he said. "But we were pretty busy. Why do you ask?"

"The Premier's son got arrested today for the Jensens' murder."

"Yeah, I heard," Rocco said. "You think those folks might be involved?"

"I don't know," I said, frowning. "At the moment, I'm grasping at straws. But I'm not convinced he had anything to do with it."

"They found some debris near the area that the cops were able to tie to him."

"Where did you hear about it?" I said.

"It was all over the news tonight," he said, then headed down the bar where some customers were waiting.

"If the kid gets convicted, the Premier can probably say goodbye to his political career," Josie said.

"Yeah, it would be impossible to survive that scandal. A son killing off his father's biggest enemy."

"And Gerald might slide right into the Premier job," Josie said, shaking her head. "Well, I guess it's good to have friends in high places, right?"

"It's always worked for my mother," I said, glancing at the front door. "Speaking of the little devil."

My mother and Gerald entered the restaurant and spotted us immediately. We exchanged greetings, then I offered my seat to her, and she sat down next to Josie. They immediately launched into a laughter-filled chat.

"Where's Rooster and Paulie?" I said to Gerald.

"Henry took them along to his weekly poker game," he said, glancing around the restaurant.

I studied his expression closely, and it eventually got his attention.

"What is it?" he said, frowning as he ran a hand over his face. "Do I have something on me?"

"No, I was just checking," I said.

"For what?"

"Your reaction to the news about William," I said.

"Darling, don't start," my mother snapped over her shoulder. "Gerald is devastated by the news."

"Thank you," Gerald said, nodding at my mother before shooting me a dirty look.

"I'm sorry, Gerald," I whispered. "That was a cheap shot."

"Yes, it was," he said, still angry. "What's the matter with you?"

"I'm just frustrated. And I'm chasing my tail on this one," I said. "I think somebody has to be setting William up."

"Of course, somebody is setting him up," Gerald said, accepting the glass of wine my mother was holding out to him. "And thanks so much for assuming I might be part of it."

"I said I was sorry, Gerald."

He took a sip then patted my hand in forgiveness and took another look around the crowded restaurant. He waved to a couple of people then took another small sip.

"But who would want to set him up?" he whispered.

"I think it could be one or more of the people who are staying at Jennifer's place," I said. "I was over there earlier today."

"How did she look?" Gerald said, going for casual.

"She looks great," I said, shrugging. "The pink hair actually looks good on her. And she's in love."

"Yes, I know that," he snapped.

An idea floated to the surface, and I studied him closely.

"That's what you had the big fight about, wasn't it?"

Gerald stared at me, then nodded and took another sip of wine.

"Sometimes, you really are too smart for your own good," he said.

"Wow, I assumed she was just another of your casual hookups," I said. "You were serious about her."

"I was."

"I hate to ask, Gerald, but aren't you a bit old for her?"

"She didn't think so," he said, glaring at me again. "And that's all that mattered."

"Yeah, okay, I get that. But she met someone else. Someone she wants to go the distance with," I said.

"She did."

"She wants to do the family thing?"

"Yes."

"And now she's talking about selling out and leaving island life behind."

"She is?" Gerald said, cocking his head at me.

"You hadn't heard?"

"How would I hear?" he said. "Jen is selling her place and moving? Let me guess. Europe."

"Yeah."

"She was always saying, let's just sell everything and move to Europe," he said, exhaling audibly. "Well, good for her. She deserves it."

"Do you know who she's in love with?"

"No, she wouldn't tell me," he said, shaking his head. "But I imagine it's someone who spends the winters down here. Knowing Jen, he's probably an artist or a musician."

"Or I guess it could be someone she met through her father."

"Highly unlikely," he said, draining his wine and setting the glass down on the bar. "She usually ran and hid from her father's friends and associates."

"That's sad," I said, frowning. "How's William doing?"

"He posted bail this afternoon," Gerald said. "But he's pretty shaky."

"I'd be shocked if he wasn't," I said, then lowered my voice so my mother couldn't hear me. "I would really like to talk with him."

"Knock yourself out," Gerald said, shrugging. "He's staying at my house."

"What?" I said, surprised.

"The press is already camped outside his condo. So, we thought my place would be a good spot for him to lay low."

"What does he think about the possibility of you taking his father's job?"

"William thinks it would be an upgrade for Cayman," Gerald said, shaking his head.

"Ouch," I said, frowning. "So, he still isn't talking to his dad?"

"Not yet," Gerald said. "I'm trying to broker a meeting between them, but so far, neither one of them is budging."

"Does the Premier think William might have done it?"

"I'm not exactly sure what the Premier thinks," Gerald said. "He and I aren't on the best of terms at the moment."

"Because he thinks you might somehow be involved?" I said, rubbing my forehead.

"I'm sure it has crossed his mind," Gerald said, glancing at my mother who was starting to pay attention to our conversation.

"That's a little paranoid, isn't it?" I said, managing a small laugh.

"It's what we politicians do," he said, grinning at me. "Especially during times like this." He leaned in close to the bar and placed a hand on my mother's shoulder. "Why don't we go sit down and have some dinner?"

"I thought you'd never ask," Josie said.

My mother and Josie slid off their stools and led the way into the dining room. Gerald placed a hand on my arm, and I stopped in my tracks.

"I'll let William know you'll be stopping by," Gerald said. "You've never been to my house before."

"I have not," I said. "But I know where it is."

"Is there anything you don't know?" he said.

"You mean, apart from who blew up that yacht?"

"Yeah, apart from that," he said, shaking his head. "Are you going to drop by tomorrow?"

"Maybe," I said. "I'm planning on spending most of the day on the water."

"You going fishing?"

"Oh, I'm sure I'll be fishing around at some point," I said, gesturing for him to lead the way.

Chapter 22

Detective Renfro listened closely to my update about my visit to Jennifer Jensen's house as he slathered sunscreen over his face and arms. He put his sunglasses back on and offered me the bottle when he was done, but I waved it off. I was already heavily layered up with a SPF strong enough to hold its own with one of Paulie's pizza ovens. But I did accept the sandwich he was holding out, and I unwrapped it and took a big bite. I washed it down with a long swig of water and leaned back against the bow railing to enjoy the breeze and my sandwich.

"You want to wet a line in while we talk?" he said. "I hear it's been a good week for wahoo."

I thought about it for a moment. Wahoo were a blast to catch, and I hadn't been fishing for several days.

"No, I don't think so," I said, shaking my head. "I'm pretty comfortable at the moment. But you go right ahead."

"Nah, it sounds like too much work," he said, cracking the top on a can of Caybrew.

"Now you're speaking my language," I said, laughing.

He smiled and stretched his legs out in front of him as he unwrapped his sandwich.

"Why do you think some of the folks staying with Jennifer might be involved?"

"Probably because nobody else makes any sense," I said, shrugging. "Except for Ramon. And since he had dinner with the security people the other night, I can make the connection."

"Only because you aren't willing to believe that William did it," Detective Renfro said through a mouthful of roasted pork and melted Swiss.

"Why would he do it?" I said, shaking my head.

"To take over a very lucrative cocaine operation is my first guess," he said.

"It's likely that the other people have the same motive."

"Sure. But William has a track record of selling dope."

"But Gerald is adamant he's no longer involved in stuff like that," I said. "He's convinced that William has turned things around and just wants to lead a quiet life."

"Then maybe he's trying to put the screws to his old man. You know, as some sort of weird payback for being a crappy father," Detective Renfro said. "And if he is, mission accomplished."

"No offense, Detective, but I think you might be letting your desire to become Police Commissioner get in the way of your better judgment."

"I can assure you, that's not it," he said, turning defensive. "We have some very solid evidence."

"Anybody could have put that debris in the water," I said.

"C'mon, Suzy," he said, laughing. "That's a major leap, even by your standards."

"Not really," I said, shaking my head. "Think about it. If someone knew the patrol boat was still out there searching for debris, all they'd need to do is toss a bunch of crap overboard. Especially if the person was familiar with the local currents."

"Pre-prepared evidence?" he said, cocking his head. "Somebody took the time to partially burn some of the wood slats from a dynamite box then embed fiberglass and feathers? And then wipe rooster blood on it?"

"It's possible," I said, my theory sounding extremely weak when voiced. I focused on my sandwich and averted eye contact. "Yeah, I can make that work."

"Wow," he said, shaking his head. "Talk about looking for a needle in the haystack."

"You said yourself it was a million to one shot that you'd find anything," I said.

"Yeah, we got very lucky," he said, focusing on his sandwich. "But planting evidence in the middle of the ocean and hoping a search party found it? Even you have to admit that idea is nuts."

"Maybe," I said, knowing he was right. "But somebody could have found it eventually. Or it would have washed up on shore somewhere."

"And whoever found it would somehow make the connection to that yacht blowing up?" he said, exasperated. "C'mon. You're better than that."

I sat quietly for a long time, then had an idea.

183

"Maybe that debris wasn't the only evidence that was planted," I said. "You know, it was just one part of an elaborate plan to set William up."

"Like what?"

"I don't know," I said, shrugging. "Maybe whoever is setting him up planted something incriminating at his company. Or in his condo."

"Well, we'll know soon enough," he said, shrugging. "I've got some guys going through both places at the moment."

"But if you find anything you're just going to consider it more evidence you can use to convict him," I said, frowning.

"Yeah, it's funny how murder investigations work," he said, laughing.

"I'm going to talk to William tomorrow," I said.

He gave my comment some thought, then nodded.

"Okay. I guess it can't hurt. But if you get anything incriminating out of him, you do know that you need to tell me, right?"

"I know that."

"Good. Try not to forget." Then he frowned at me, confused. "He's willing to talk to you without his lawyer present?"

"According to Gerald, he is," I said, draining the last of my water. "Which I take as additional proof that he's innocent. You know, an indication that he has nothing to hide."

184

"Yeah, okay. Knock yourself out," Detective Renfro said, then swallowed a mouthful of beer. "New topic."

"Ramon."

"What about him?" he said, finishing his sandwich.

"He doesn't strike me as someone capable of masterminding something like this," I said.

"That seems pretty obvious," Detective Renfro said, nodding his agreement. "One more reason to like William for it."

"But Ramon does seem like a guy who'd be a good follower," I said. "For the right price."

"No offense, Suzy, but I think you might be letting the fact that Ramon ran illegal cockfights get in the way of your better judgment," he said, giving me a smug smile.

"Touché," I said, conceding the point. "I would like to see him get everything that's coming to him."

"I'm sure you would, but we don't have anything on him. Apart from the cockfighting, of course. Our surveillance hasn't turned up anything."

"He's probably laying low for the moment," I said. "He was at dinner with those people the other night. Rocco said their conversation got heated a couple of times."

"Suzy, if I start arresting people for eating dinner, you and Josie are in a world of hurt," he said, finding his own joke very funny.

I grabbed an ice-cold beer from the cooler as I waited for him to stop laughing.

"I think it's time to have a chat with him," I said, then nodded at how good the first sip tasted in the hot sun.

"What do you want to talk to Ramon about?"

"I have no idea," I said, shaking my head.

"Well, I'm glad to hear that you have a plan," Detective Renfro said. "You can't drop by unannounced at his house or where he works. That's bound to make him suspicious. And that would make our surveillance even harder."

"So, you do still have him under surveillance?"

"Of course," Detective Renfro said, yawning. "It's an ongoing investigation."

"You guys are still convinced the cockfighting and the smuggling are connected?"

"Well, *connected* might be a bit of an overstatement," he said, shaking his head. "But we do think they at least intersect in some way."

"I need a way to bump into Ramon," I said. "You know, a chance encounter."

"I know where you're going with this, and it's not a good idea, Suzy," he said, staring at me.

"I heard that Ramon likes to drop by some dive bar after work," I said.

"I knew that was where you were going," he said.

"Great minds think alike," I said, grinning at him.

"He does stop by there most days. But I wouldn't recommend you going anywhere near that place. That bar can get pretty rough."

"I'll be fine," I said, staring out at the ocean. "Wouldn't you like to get some information from Ramon you can use?"

"We would," he said. "But if something were to happen to you, I'd hate having to explain why I didn't do everything I could to stop you from going there."

"Yeah, I get that. That would be tough to explain. Especially with you being so close to that new job, right?" I said, then immediately regretted saying it.

"That's a cheap shot," he whispered. "Why can't you just accept the fact that I don't want to see you get hurt?"

"I'm sorry," I said, crushed by my borderline-cruel comment. "I don't know why I say stuff like that."

"Forget it," he said, shaking his head. "You've said worse. And by now, I'm pretty used to it."

"I'm really sorry, Detective," I said. "When my brain gets overloaded, and the adrenaline starts flowing, I have a hard time controlling my mouth. For what it's worth, I hope you get the job. I think you'd make an excellent police commissioner."

"Now, you're just sucking up," he said, laughing.

"Yeah, how am I doing?" I said, laughing along with him.

"Let me know when you plan on dropping by the bar," he said, staring at me to emphasize the point. "I'll make sure we have a couple of guys there."

"How will I know who they are?"

"You won't," he said. "But if anything does happen, you'll know who they are in a hurry."

"Okay," I said, nodding.

"And one more thing," he said, crushing his empty can and tossing it onto the seat next to him.

"What's that?" I said, draining the last of my beer.

"Take some backup along with you."

"Backup?"

"Yeah, and from what I saw at the cockfight, your friend Rooster would be perfect."

"He does like to see how some of the locals live," I said, shrugging.

"Well, get ready. Because you're both in for a real treat."

Chapter 23

Gerald's house was less than fifteen minutes from our place in a planned community just north of Georgetown called Camana Bay. I always thought calling it a bay was a bit of a misnomer since its western edge set on a stretch of Seven Mile Beach, and to the east were a series of interconnected canals that eventually worked their way out to the ocean. As such, the canals aside, as far as I was concerned, it was still pretty much all oceanfront. The entire community was upscale and included a ton of modern amenities that offered residents what Josie considered a self-contained lifestyle. To be more accurate, she called it Bubble World. We occasionally dropped by to catch a movie or go shopping when we were looking for something to do other than lounge by the pool with the dogs or take the boat out. Although Camana Bay was gorgeous and well-maintained, the overall impression I got every time I visited reminded me more of something I'd see in Florida or parts of California, and it didn't have the funky Caribbean vibe I'd come to love.

But obviously Camana Bay was to Gerald's liking, and I turned into the driveway that led to a sprawling, single-story residence with a great view of the canal. I got out of the jeep and took the place in with an admiring stare. I headed for the front door, rang the bell, and looked around again as I waited. The door opened, and a barefoot man somewhere in his late twenties wearing beach shorts and a tee shirt greeted me with a smile. But he looked tired, and I couldn't miss the stress that seemed etched on his face.

"Suzy, right?"

"That's me," I said, extending my hand. "It's nice to finally meet you, William. I've heard a lot about you."

"I'm sure you have," he said, nodding. "Come on in."

I followed him into the house and down a tiled hallway lined with photos of Gerald and various celebrities and dignitaries.

"I call this Gerald's Walk of Fame Redux," he said, managing a small laugh when he noticed me slowing down to check out some of the identically-framed photos.

"He must have run out of room at his office," I said, remembering the walls in Gerald's office that overflowed with framed photos.

"That's right," William said, giving me a coy smile. "I heard you've been in his office a couple of times."

I let his gentle jab pass without comment and followed him as he made a right turn. We went through a set of sliding glass doors and ended up on an outside patio that butted up against the pool. We sat down at a small table, and he poured me a glass of iced tea from a pitcher.

"I'm sorry," he said, frowning. "I didn't even bother to ask if you wanted tea. Perhaps, a glass of wine or a beer?"

"No, this is great," I said, taking a long sip as I glanced around the pool area and yard. "I see Gerald all the time, and I can't believe I've never been here before."

"Yes, he's told me a lot about you," William said. "He's been in the house for about a year. It's nice, but I prefer more traditional Caribbean. If I wanted this, I would have never left Miami."

"You were in Miami?"

"I went to college there for a few years, then decided it wasn't for me. But I stayed there for another year until…"

"Until you came back here and got busted for smuggling dope," I said. "Yeah, I heard all about it."

"Truly a bad decision on my part," he said. "I'm very fortunate to be sitting here with you at the moment."

"Yes," I said, nodding. "I'm sure you are."

William chuckled and stared at me.

"Is that a shot about how lucky I am that my father can pull some strings when necessary?"

"Let's call it an observation," I said, grinning back at him over the top of my glass.

He laughed and draped a leg over his knee then lit a cigarette and blew smoke downwind.

"Gerald said you were a *truly unique* individual. I'm beginning to get a glimpse of what he was talking about. You don't pull a lot of punches, do you?"

"I've never been much of a dancer, William," I said, shrugging. "I'm more of a straight ahead kind of girl."

"Got it," he said, tapping his cigarette against the ashtray on the table. "Gerald also said that you may be able to help me. He said you have a gift when it comes to figuring out complex problems, particularly those associated with criminal behavior."

"Most days, it feels like more of a curse," I said. "But I am pretty good at things like this."

"So, what are your thoughts on this one?"

"I'm starting to develop a few ideas, but I'm not comfortable sharing them just yet," I said, sliding my chair into a patch of shade. "I need to ask you some questions."

"Of course."

"How well did you know Jack and Jill Jensen?"

"Quite well," he said, shrugging. "Especially when I was younger. But after their falling out with my father, I didn't see much of the Jensens."

"What was their fight about?" I said, folding my legs underneath me on the chair.

"Politics and money, primarily," William said, crushing out his cigarette. "Mr. Jensen felt that my father had pulled the rug out from under him and made him a public laughingstock."

"But that must have been before your dad became Premier, right?"

"Way before," William said, staring out at the pool. "My father and Mr. Jensen were still working as lawyers for a local firm. Actually, what happened between him and the Jensens was what launched my dad's political career."

"That was his Shine the Light campaign, right?"

"Very good. You've been doing your homework," William said, nodding.

"That campaign was all about bringing what your father considered to be some of the more unsavory aspects of how things worked down here out from under the rocks and into the light," I said, helping myself to more tea. He waved off my offer of a refill, and I set the pitcher down then sat back and waited.

"It was. And Jack Jensen was the poster child for that campaign. Mr. Jensen never forgave my father and told him in no uncertain terms that he'd get even at some point," he said. "My father's campaign was very popular with a lot of the local residents. Most of the financial people and developers hated it."

"And I imagine they weren't very fond of your father, either," I said.

"At first, no," William said. "But my father has proven to be quite prophetic about the future. He saw the need to clean things up long before anyone else did. Even before the countries who would eventually be applying the pressure ever recognized the need to do it."

"Countries like the UK and the States, right?"

"Pretty much," he said, shrugging. "Since we're an Overseas British Territory, obviously the UK has a lot of clout down here. And I'm sure I don't need to explain how much

193

influence the Americans have when they decide they want something done."

"The UK and the States both wanted a lot of the money schemes cleaned up, right?" I said.

"9/11 changed a lot of things dramatically around the world," William said. "And Cayman certainly wasn't immune."

"But the place still has a reputation for being a financial haven," I said.

"Again, my father proved himself to be quite prescient when it comes to that," he said. "And Gerald as well."

"I'm not following," I said, leaning forward.

"Gerald and my father have been instrumental in making sure that people are still able to do certain things with their money, but do it in a way that doesn't attract a lot of what they consider to be *unnecessary oversight*."

"It sounds complicated," I said, frowning.

"It's *very* complicated," he said, laughing. "And that's why it works as well as it does."

"You're saying your father was able to maintain his reputation as a man of the people without losing the support of the big money people who make this place run?"

"Suzy," William said. "My father is a lot of things, but he's not an idiot. And as I'm sure I don't have to tell you, neither is Gerald."

"No, you don't," I said, then drifted off for a few moments to be alone with my thoughts. "Who do you think is trying to set you up?"

"I wish I knew," he said with a tired shrug. "It's obviously someone who's trying to ruin my father's career. Why else would anybody want to kill the Jensens and try to pin it on me?"

"That question has been driving me nuts for several days," I said. "You think it could be someone who's also making a play for Jensen's dope business?"

"That thought has certainly crossed my mind," he said, lighting another cigarette.

"Those things will kill you," I said, nodding at the cigarette.

"They're the least of my concerns at the moment," he said, exhaling smoke.

"Fair point," I said. "Did you know that Jensen was smuggling coke?"

"I did not," he said, firmly. "I was shocked when I heard about it. But given what I'd heard about his gambling problem, it probably shouldn't have surprised me."

"How did you know about his gambling?"

"Small island," he said, shrugging it off.

"Sure, sure," I said, then shifted gears. "Talk to me about Ramon."

"Ramon?" William said, cocking his head at me. "What about him?"

"Do you think he could be involved?"

William gave it some thought, then nodded.

"Sure, it's possible," William said. "For the right amount of money, I'm pretty sure Ramon would sell his own mother."

"He works for you, right?"

"Not anymore," William said, shaking his head. "He quit several months ago. It's too bad he did. He's a good worker."

"Good at blowing things up?" I said, then polished off the last of my tea.

"Actually, I'm the one who handles all of our demolition jobs," he said. "It's dangerous work, and I'm a bit of a control freak."

"But Ramon could have learned how it's done, right?"

"Sure, it's really not that difficult to blow stuff up," he said. "I've got at least a dozen people working for me who know how to do it. The hard part is only blowing up what you want and leaving everything else intact."

"But you wouldn't have to worry about that way out in the middle of the ocean, right?"

"No, you wouldn't," he said, shaking his head. "And that yacht must have been packed to the gills with explosives for it to disintegrate the way it did."

"Explosives from your company," I said, raising an eyebrow.

"That's the way it looks," he said, taking a long drag then exhaling a cloud of smoke that quickly disappeared in the breeze.

196

"You didn't know that some of your inventory had gone missing?"

"No, I didn't. And that's my fault," William said. "I haven't been paying a lot of attention to my company recently."

"Have you lost interest in it?" I said, again sliding my chair a few feet to my right into the shade.

"Actually, I have," he said, smiling at my attempt to duck the sun. "My plan is to sell it. But that's not the reason I haven't been paying attention."

"Okay," I said, frowning as I waited for him to continue.

"I haven't been paying attention because I'm in love," he said, beaming.

"That's a good reason," I said, laughing as I reached for the pitcher of tea. "Who's the lucky girl?"

"Me."

I turned toward the direction of the voice and almost dropped the pitcher. I stared in disbelief at the woman with pink hair who was wearing a bathing suit and leaning against one of the sliding glass doors.

"Jennifer?" I finally managed.

"Hi, Suzy," she said, strolling toward us and pausing to give William a kiss on the cheek before sitting down and helping herself to one of his cigarettes. "I thought I'd finally kicked the habit, but then he got me started again."

"Yeah, right," William said, laughing. "Now, it's my fault."

"Surprised, huh?" she said, grinning at me.

"That's a word for it," I said, glancing back and forth at them. "I'm very confused."

"Join the club," Jennifer said.

"But Gerald said he had no idea who you were involved with," I said.

"He doesn't," Jennifer said. "But we're going to tell him tonight when he gets home. It's time."

"Does your father know?" I said, staring at William, still baffled.

"No. I was getting ready to tell him, and then all this stuff happened," he said. "I'm afraid we're going to have to wait a bit longer before I spring it on him. He's got enough on his plate at the moment."

"Like keeping you from being convicted of murder and saving his political career?" I said.

"Yes, but probably not in that order," William said.

"Don't be like that, Will," Jennifer said. "I'm sure your dad is doing everything he can to help you."

"Yeah, you might be right," William said, reaching for her hand. "But we both know he's going to blame me for everything that happens to him. And there goes any chance of reconciling with him."

"You don't know that," Jennifer said, squeezing his hand.

"Did your folks know you two were together?" I said.

"Yes, I told them about a month ago," Jennifer said. "What a mistake that was. They threatened to disown me if I didn't break it off. I basically told them to stick it."

"And?" I said, staring at her.

"And now it doesn't matter what they thought," she said with a shrug. "They're gone, and as soon as we get Will cleared of these ridiculous charges, we're leaving and probably never coming back."

"I can't wait," William said, draining the last of his tea. "But if I am convicted, you'll wait for me, right?"

"I'll leave you a forwarding address," she said, then gave him a deep, long kiss that left me red-faced. "That's the least I can do."

"You're all heart," he said, laughing.

"I'm going to take a dip and cool off," she said. "It was nice seeing you, Suzy."

"Yeah, you too," I said, as she strolled toward the pool, dove in and began churning laps. I looked at William who was watching her with a contented smile. "I should get going."

"Do you have any ideas about what to do next?" he said, finally taking his eyes off her.

"I thought I might have a little chat with Ramon," I said, getting to my feet.

"Okay," he said, shielding his eyes with a hand as he glanced up at me. "Let me know how that goes. And if there's anything I can do, just ask."

"Will do," I said. "But for now, it's probably a good idea if you and Jennifer just stay here and keep a low profile."

"Oh, no," he said, sneaking a glance at the pool. "Not the briar patch."

Chapter 24

I headed home and found Josie and Chef Claire sprawled out in lounge chairs next to the pool playing with the dogs. They both reached down to retrieve the tennis balls and fired them back into the pool. I got halfway across the lawn before the dogs spotted me, and they forgot about the balls momentarily as they climbed out of the pool and raced to drench me with a cool shower. I spent a few minutes petting all of them, then headed toward Josie and Chef Claire. The dogs dove back in the pool in search of the tennis balls that were gently bobbing in the water.

"Welcome home," Josie said, laughing as she tossed me a towel. "You probably should have changed before you came out."

"Yeah, good call," I said, wiping my face. "Where's the rest of the gang?"

"Your mom said she had some errands to run, and Rooster went fishing with Paulie and Rocco," Chef Claire said. "I hope they have some luck. I've got a new recipe for smoked wahoo I'm dying to try out."

"Did you get a chance to speak with William?" Josie said.

"I did," I said, sitting down on one of the loungers. "It started out fine, but it turned weird at the end."

"Weird how?" Josie said, sitting up to slather on another layer of sunscreen.

"He's in love," I said.

"Okay," Josie said. "It has been known to happen. Was his girlfriend at the house?"

"She was," I said, shaking my head. "And you'll never guess who it is."

"How many guesses do we get?" Chef Claire said.

"As many as you want," I said. "You'll never get it."

"Then you should probably just tell us," Chef Claire said.

"Jennifer Jensen."

"The daughter of the people who got blown up?" Josie said, frowning. "That is weird."

"So, she not only dropped Gerald for a younger guy, she dumped him for his godson?" Chef Claire said. "How do you think he's going to react to that news?"

"At first, probably not well," I said, reaching down to pet Chloe and grab the tennis ball she had dropped at my feet. "Don't you dare shake on me again."

I did my best to shield myself from the torrent of water then fired the ball back into the pool. I wiped myself off again and stretched out on the lounger.

"Jennifer said that her parents threatened to disown her if she didn't break it off," I said, glancing over at them.

"Maybe everyone underestimated just how much bad blood there was between the two families," Josie said.

"Yeah, William said that Jensen never forgave his father for what he did to him," I said.

"What did he do?" Chef Claire said.

"He made an example of him then used it as the centerpiece of his first political campaign," I said. "It sounded like it was some sort of shady financial deal."

"So, we've got some sort of Romeo and Juliet thing going on?" Chef Claire said.

"Yeah, that pretty much sums it up," I said.

"You don't think that the daughter might have been involved with the yacht blowing up, do you?" Josie said.

"She wouldn't have done that to her parents. Estranged is one thing, but that's just sick."

"We've seen stranger things," Josie said.

"Yes, I suppose we have," I said, nodding.

"And she is inheriting everything," Josie said.

"Maybe it was some weird sort of payback," Chef Claire said. "Revenge is always a good motive."

"If I hadn't seen the way they are with each other, I probably could have jumped to that conclusion," I said.

"Just so you could say you got your workout in, right?" Josie said.

"Funny," I said, making a face at her. "But as soon as I saw them together, I knew there's no way she could have done it. You know, since there was a good chance that William might have been blamed for it."

"Maybe she didn't think there was any way that would happen," Chef Claire said.

"But if that were the case, she would have felt guilty about it," I said. "And I didn't pick a trace of that. They're a couple of lovebirds."

"So, where does that leave you?" Chef Claire said.

"Chasing my tail," I said. "I need to talk with Gerald at some point."

"But not until after he hears about William and Jennifer, right?" Josie said.

"Yeah, there's no way I'm going to be the one who breaks the news to him," I said. "He's going to need some time to process it."

"That makes sense," Josie said, wiping her hands on a towel. "Chef Claire and I were talking about catching a late afternoon movie, then heading to the restaurant for dinner."

"You're taking the night off?" I said to Chef Claire.

"I am," she said. "I'm doing everything I can to work myself out of a job."

"Don't do anything crazy," Josie said, giving her a mock stern look. "You want to join us?"

"No, thanks. But maybe I'll manage to make it to dinner. Rooster and I have something to do later on."

"Like what?" Josie said, glancing over at me.

"We're going out for drinks."

"Should I even ask where you're going?" Josie said.

"Probably not," I said, shaking my head.

"Just so I'll have plausible deniability in case your mom is looking for you?"

"You're on fire today."

Chapter 25

I pulled into small dirt parking lot next to the makeshift structure constructed of wood, cinderblock, and corrugated tin. It was painted lime green with purple trim, and a block-letter sign hung precariously from the top of the verandah and swayed gently in the breeze. We were in the northwest corner of Grand Cayman in an area called West Bay that was less than ten miles north of our place on Seven Mile Beach. Although the area had a residential feel to it, the inexorable creep of development and high-end housing was definitely making its presence known. But for the time being, the bar called *Neptune's Landing* had managed to escape what so many call progress, and it sat on a side street nestled among a small stretch of shops selling tee shirts and assorted tourist tchotchke.

Rooster and I climbed out of the jeep and took a few moments to take the place in before frowning at each other.

"Are you thinking what I am?" Rooster said.

"I think Detective Renfro must have a different definition of what constitutes a dive bar," I said. "This place isn't bad at all."

"Yeah, I kinda like it," Rooster said, nodding his approval. "It looks like our kind of place. Maybe the detective has gotten spoiled hanging out at all the resorts."

"If Detective Renfro ever comes for a visit, we should take him to The Outer Limit," I said, laughing. "You know, to broaden his horizons."

The Outer Limit was a notorious drinking establishment not far from Clay Bay that was as close to the epitome of *dive bar* I'd ever been in. Rooster chuckled at my comment then turned serious.

"So, how do you want to play this?" he said.

"We should probably go in separately."

"Okay," Rooster said, glancing around at the sparse, late-afternoon crowd that was sitting outside under the covered verandah.

"Detective Renfro said there would be a couple of undercover cops here," I said.

"I'm sure I'll be able to pick them out," Rooster said. "How are you going to handle Ramon?"

"I thought I'd just start with my usual," I said.

"When in doubt, poke the bear?"

"An oldie but a goodie," I said, grinning back at him as I headed up the small set of steps.

I entered the small, dark bar and paused in the doorway and glanced around. The windows were open, and two overhead fans were doing their best to keep the air circulating and deal with a thick cloud of cigarette and cigar smoke that hovered. There were about a dozen tables, half of them occupied, and several men lined the bar either chatting in pairs or hunched over alone with their thoughts. I spotted a large man with his back to me, and when he turned his head to get the bartender's attention, I caught a glimpse of a gold hoop earring. I headed for the bar and wedged myself in next to Ramon. At first, he grudgingly gave me enough room to get my elbows on the bar, but when he realized I was a woman, he took a step to his right and did a half-turn and beamed at me.

"Well, hello there," he said, ogling me from head to toe. "Can I buy you a drink?"

"Only if you let me return the favor," I said, extending my hand. "I'm Suzy."

"It's nice to meet you, Suzy," he said. "I'm *Ramon*."

He pronounced his name as if it should register with me. Maybe, like Sting or Madonna, he only needed the one name for people to know who he was. Perhaps organizing cockfights was enough to put him on the celebrity A-list in the circles he traveled.

"What would you like?" he said, snapping his fingers at the bartender, a trait I found incredibly annoying and disrespectful to service workers.

"Please don't do that," I said, frowning at him.

"Do what?" he said, confused.

"Wisdom tends to grow in proportion to one's awareness of one's ignorance," I said, glancing down at several empty shot glasses lined up in front of him. "What are you drinking?"

"Beer with rum chasers," he said, still trying to process my comment about his lack of self-awareness.

"I think I'll just go with a beer," I said, getting ready to make my initial cast. "I'm not a big fan of rum."

"You're not much for the hard stuff, huh?" he said.

"Oh, I've been known to drink liquor," I said, tossing my line out. "But I doubt if they have my favorite here."

"And just what would your favorite be?" Ramon said, leaning closer and exuding a scent that was a combination of sweat, booze, and what I thought was cement.

"Arrack," I said, casually tossing it out for him to digest.

Ramon twitched, quickly recovered, then forced a smile.

"Arrack? What the heck is that?"

"It's a liquor that's common in a lot of countries in Asia," I said, returning the smile. "But my favorite is one that's made in Sri Lanka."

That got another mild twitch out of Ramon, and his eyes narrowed.

"Sri Lanka?" he said. "You ever been there?"

"No," I said, maintaining my smile. "I just like their booze. Have you been there?"

"I couldn't find the place on a map," he said, then ordered my beer and another round for himself.

It was a good response to use to avoid answering the question, and I put Ramon down as a definite maybe when it came to whether he had visited the place. The bartender set my beer down in front of me, and I took a long sip of the ice-cold Caybrew.

"That hits the spot," I said, taking another sip. "It's hot today."

"It's always hot. You should try working in it all day," Ramon said, tossing back his shot of rum and washing it down with what had to be half his beer.

"What do you do for work?" I said, going for casual.

"At the moment, I'm back in construction," he said, draining his beer and waving to the bartender. "I'm thirsty."

"You deserve it," I said, turning sympathetic. "Working in that hot sun all day."

The bartender returned with Ramon's drinks and set them down in front of him and glanced at me.

"No, I'm good for the moment," I said, reaching into my pocket for cash. I handed the bartender more than enough to cover a couple of rounds. "Here you go. Get one for yourself while you're at it."

"Thanks," the bartender said, then wandered off.

"I do like a woman who buys drinks," Ramon said, reaching for his rum.

"Happy to do it," I said, beaming at him. "And I do like a working man. Construction, huh?"

"Just for now," he said, stifling a burp. "I'll be transitioning into something new soon."

"A career change?" I said, nodding as I took another sip. "Interesting. What are you going to be doing next?"

"Well, I was about to get into the import-export business, but that's hit a snag," he said, his eyes starting to glaze over.

"Oh, I hate when that happens."

"Tell me about it," Ramon said, tossing back his shot of rum and immediately waving for another.

"Maybe we should just ask the bartender to leave the bottle," I said, tossing some more cash on the bar.

"What's your deal?" he said, glancing back and forth at me and the money. "You rich or something? Or maybe you're just a tourist who likes to sample some of the local attractions."

He puffed up and leered at me. I almost threw up in my mouth, but recovered and took a long swig of Caybrew.

"No, just looking to kill a few hours before dinner," I said, then glanced at the bartender. "Just leave the bottle, so we don't have to keep bothering you. But on second thought, I think I am going to need another beer. Thanks."

Ramon poured himself a shot, tossed it back, then refilled the glass and left it sitting in front of him.

"So, your plans to work in the import-export business went south, huh?"

"Yeah," he said, deflated. "And those people better pay me what they owe me pretty soon, or we're gonna have a problem."

"They owe you money even though you haven't started working for them?"

"I did a few odd jobs for them," Ramon said, deflecting. Then he decided a new topic of conversation was called for. "So, what's your deal? What do you do?"

"I spend most of my time working with dogs and food," I said with a shrug.

"You work in dog food?" he said, puzzled.

"No. Dogs *and* food," I said. "I'm involved in a couple of restaurants. And I run a dog business. You know, veterinary services, dog rescue, stuff like that."

"Hmmm," he said, giving it some serious thought.

"I love it," I said. "Especially the rescue side. Why, just the other day, we rescued the most gorgeous poodle you've ever seen."

"You don't say," Ramon said, setting the shot of rum he was about to inhale back down on the bar. "A poodle, huh?"

"Yes. She was very lucky to get off that boat before it blew up," I whispered.

Ramon gave me a long stare, then tossed his shot back and washed it down with half a beer.

"The dog got off the boat?" he said, staring off at a spot behind the bar.

"Yes," I said, nodding. "Unfortunately, the people who were on it didn't."

"Yeah, I think I heard something about a boat blowing up the other day."

"I'm sure you did," I said, glancing over at him.

"What?"

"I mean, how could you not have? It was all over the news."

"Oh, yeah, sure. That's where I heard it," Ramon said, toying with the bottle of rum, apparently unsure if he should have any more.

"And I just heard that the police have arrested the Premier's son for it," I said, shaking my head in disbelief. "Can you believe that?"

"I guess anything is possible," Ramon said, giving me a wary stare.

"The police apparently found some debris that ties him to the explosion," I said. "Bad luck for him, huh?"

"I guess," Ramon said with a shrug. "But I really wouldn't have a clue."

Now that he was on the defensive, I had a choice to back off or go full speed ahead. I glanced around the bar and noticed Rooster staring back at me. Then he looked away, and I followed his eyes to two men who were doing their best to look like a couple of tourists enjoying an afternoon cocktail. They were sitting at a table near the bar, and when my eyes landed on one of them, he gave me a slight nod of his head. Since I had more than enough backup, I decided to push Ramon a bit more.

"They said on the news that the guy they arrested has a construction company that specializes in demolition," I said, staring deep into Ramon's eyes. "Hey, you work in construction. Maybe you know him."

213

"No, I can't say that I do," Ramon said, then placed his hand on my forearm and left it there. "You seem like a woman who knows how to party."

"Oh, does it show?" I said, going for coy.

"It's written all over your face," he said, fiddling with one of the gold hoops with his free hand.

"I've been known to cut loose from time to time," I said. "But from what I've heard, most of the local supply took a serious hit when that boat went up."

"What?" he said, his eyes going wide.

"But you're the kind of guy who wouldn't let that stop him, right, *Ramon*? I'm sure you have lots of ways to get around that problem. I mean, a guy like you must have all sorts of connections with the right people."

He glared at me then his expression morphed into a huge smile.

"Say, why don't we get out of here and go someplace more comfortable?"

"Oh, I don't know, Ramon," I said, taking a sip. "I'm pretty comfortable here at the moment."

"I'm sure we can do a lot better than this place," he said, starting to squeeze my arm.

"Ow. Please, stop that, Ramon," I said, flinching. "That hurts."

"Oh, I'm sorry," he said, releasing some of the pressure without letting go of my arm. "Say, why don't we go to my place? It's not far from here."

"Why would I want to do that?" I said, grimacing.

"Well, to party, of course. I'd love to have a chat with you in private," he said, ratcheting up the pressure on my arm.

"I bet you would," I said, trying to get my arm free. "I should probably warn you that I bit the last guy who did that."

"Oh, you like to get rough, huh?" His face morphed again, this time into an expression that made the hairs on the back of my neck stand up. "I'm sure I'll be able to accommodate you. Let's get out of here. You'll find my place very interesting."

"Interesting?" I said with a cold stare. "Why, is there a cockfight there tonight?"

Ramon recoiled, intensified his glare, then tried to squeeze the life out of my arm.

"Who the hell are you?"

"I'm Suzy," I said, again struggling to get my arm free.

Ramon started to turn away from the bar and pull me toward the door when he was thwarted by a large presence standing directly behind him.

"Excuse me," Ramon said to Rooster. "You're in my way."

"Well done. You got it in one. Maybe you aren't a total idiot," Rooster said without emotion. "Let go of her arm."

"This is none of your business," Ramon said. "The lady and I have a few things to talk about."

"Let go of her arm."

"And if I don't?" Ramon said, making a big mistake by asking that question.

Rooster effortlessly snatched the offending hand free, bent the index finger back until I heard it pop, then he grabbed Ramon by the back of the neck and bounced his forehead hard once against the edge of the bar. Apart from the force of the blow and the fact that the object was a large bald head, Rooster's movement was reminiscent of how one might crack an egg. I suppose Ramon would have screamed from the pain of his broken finger if he hadn't dropped like a rock, unconscious.

Everyone inside the bar initially focused on the commotion, then lost interest and went back to what they'd been doing. I glanced over at the two cops who were sipping their beers as they watched the scene play out. The bartender peered over the bar at Ramon who was splayed out on the floor. Then he gave Rooster a blank stare, apparently waiting for him to speak first. Rooster showed his palms to the bartender then reached into his pocket and tossed some money on the bar.

"We'll be leaving now," Rooster said. "Why don't you buy a round for everybody then keep the change?"

"I'll do that," the bartender said. "But you might not want to come back for a while. Ramon's a total jerk, but he does have some pretty rough friends who don't mind mixing it up."

"Thanks for the tip," Rooster said, giving the bartender a small wave as he led me by the elbow toward the door. When we

216

were outside, he took his hand away and grinned at me. "What did you say that set him off?"

"I worked in a cockfighting reference," I said, rubbing my sore forearm. "He wanted to take me back to his place. And I don't think he had romance in mind."

"Maybe the engagement ring scared him off," Rooster said with a laugh as he hopped into the passenger seat.

"I was just about to deck him and see if I could leave a diamond imprint on his face," I said, starting the jeep. "But thanks for bailing me out."

"No problem. That's why I was there."

"Interesting that the cops just let it play out," I said, pulling into traffic and heading for home. "I'm glad. Getting arrested again wouldn't have gone over well."

"No, it wouldn't," he said. "But they weren't going to blow their cover unless they absolutely had to. So, what did Ramon have to say for himself?"

"Oh, he's an absolute delight," I said, glancing over at him. "And he certainly does like to tell lies."

"That might come in handy."

"I'm counting on it."

Chapter 26

"Was all this cloak and dagger stuff really necessary? I don't know why you just didn't come to my office."

"I'm never going back to your office, Gerald," I said, glancing around the empty dining room.

Our restaurant was closed during the day on Wednesdays so that Chef Claire and some of her staff could visit the weekly farmer's market to shop for locally grown products. But she had begged off today after kindly agreeing to my request to use the restaurant for a private lunch meeting with Gerald and Detective Renfro. She then decided it would be the perfect time to test out some of the new recipes she'd been toying with and was in the kitchen putting together a tasting menu for us to sample.

Our clandestine meeting was part of Detective Renfro's ongoing need to keep my involvement in the investigation quiet, and since my mother hadn't asked me a single question about what I was up to, I certainly wasn't going to argue with the detective's strategy. But he hadn't arrived yet, and I was sitting across from a confused and forlorn Gerald who had his suit jacket off and his crisp white sleeves rolled up. He used a finger to stir the ice in his glass of tea as he stared down at the table. I frowned at what he was doing but said nothing.

"You look like your dog died," I said, taking a sip of my tea.

"I don't have a dog." he said, not bothering to make eye contact.

"Figure of speech, Gerald," I said. "But maybe you should think about getting one."

"With my schedule, it probably wouldn't be fair to the dog," he said, finally looking up at me. "I still can't believe it."

"What's really bothering you, Gerald?" I said, starting to lose patience with my good friend who'd been pouting since we'd sat down. "The fact that she chose someone else, or the fact that neither one of them told you about it?"

"Why both, of course," he said, then managed a soft chuckle. "It was just a shock to come home and see them together in the pool."

"William was worried you'd tell his father that he was in love with the daughter of his sworn enemy?"

"That's his story," Gerald said, finally removing his finger from his glass. Then he took a big drink.

"That's disgusting," I said, scowling.

"Hey, it's my finger, and it's my tea," he said as stuck his finger back in the glass and resumed stirring. "Whatever germs are there are all mine."

"Maybe it wasn't your age that drove Jennifer into the arms of another man," I said, nodding at the swirling ice cubes in his glass.

"Funny," he said, stirring faster. "Look, I'm glad they're happy. I really am. I just wish they hadn't blindsided me with it."

"I'm sure they felt like they didn't have any other choice," I said. "You aren't going to tell the Premier, are you?"

"No, I'm not. I gave William my word."

"You're a good guy, Gerald," I said, patting his dry hand.

We both looked up when we heard the front door open. But instead of seeing Detective Renfro, Josie strolled in and removed her sunglasses, spotted us, then wandered over to our table.

"What are you doing here?" I said.

"You think I'm going to stay home while Chef Claire is testing out some new recipes?" she said. "I offered to help serve and wash dishes."

"Unbelievable," I said, laughing.

"Like I'm going to miss her first batch of smoked wahoo tacos," Josie said. "She said she's using a mint-sage tartar sauce on them that will take your breath away."

"Reading a menu takes your breath away," I said. Then I gave it some thought. "Sage is an odd choice, isn't it?"

"Smoked wahoo tastes a lot like turkey," Josie said.

"Good for the smoked wahoo," I said, frowning. "It's still fish."

"More for me," she said, giving us a finger wave as she headed off. "I'll be in the kitchen."

"Oh, waitress," I said, calling after her in my best sing-song voice.

Josie stopped in her tracks, then slowly wheeled around and glared at me.

"What?"

"I dropped my fork. Would you mind bringing me a new one?"

"So, that's how you're going to play it, huh?" she said.

"I have no idea what you're talking about," I said, grinning at her.

Before the swinging door that led into the kitchen came to a stop, the front door opened again, and Detective Renfro entered. He headed for our table and sat down between us.

"Sorry, I'm late," he said, scanning the table. "Where are the menus?"

"Chef Claire is doing a tasting menu for us," I said.

"Cool," he said, groaning as he arched his back and stretched his arms over his head. "I've been spending too much time sitting."

"I assume you've been out fighting crime all morning from the comfort of your car?" I said with a grin.

"Actually, I swung by the hospital to have a chat with one of the nurses," Detective Renfro said. "Ramon was released this morning."

"He was in the hospital overnight?" I said, frowning. "Rooster didn't hit him that hard."

"That's not what the undercover guys said," Detective Renfro said. "The hospital decided to keep him in for

221

observation. He's got a concussion. Not to mention what the nurse called a decorative horizontal crease running the length of his forehead."

Gerald frowned and glanced back and forth at us, confused.

"Ramon got handsy with me, and Rooster bounced his head off the bar," I said, shrugging. "I guess Ramon is lucky it had a rounded edge."

"Yes, and also fortunate you didn't bite him," Detective Renfro said. "You know, based on your usual reaction when people get *handsy* with you."

"Good one," I said, making a face at him. "Is Ramon filing charges?"

"No, actually he didn't even want to talk about the incident. He played it down and said it was just a little argument between friends."

"Okay, that pretty much confirms my suspicions," I said, nodding.

"Which are?" Detective Renfro said.

"That he blew up the yacht," I said.

"That's a bit of a leap, wouldn't you say?" the detective said, pouring himself a glass of tea.

"If you buy the idea that William didn't do it, he's the most logical suspect," I said.

"This would probably be a good time for you to give me an update on what you and Ramon talked about," Detective Renfro said.

I spent the next few minutes giving them the summary version then sat back and waited for questions.

"You said he seemed surprised that the poodle made it off the boat?" Detective Renfro said.

"He did," I said. "He tried to deflect his comment right away, but you couldn't miss the tone of his voice. And that can only mean one thing, right?"

"That he knew the dog was on the boat," the detective said after giving it some thought. "But he obviously knew the Jensens, and I'm sure he was aware that the dog went everywhere with them."

"Yeah, but his reaction still seemed strange."

"He really said he didn't know William?" Gerald said. "Ramon worked for him for a couple of years."

"That was right around the time when Ramon started getting suspicious," I said. "I imagine he decided to just clam up and lie to me. I was definitely starting to annoy him."

"I'm shocked," Gerald said, smiling at Detective Renfro.

"Yeah, imagine that," the detective said, laughing.

The kitchen door swung open, and Josie entered the dining room carrying a tray. She set it down in the middle of the table, and I did a quick survey of the contents before looking up at her.

"Why thank you, waitress," I said, beaming at Josie. "Would you mind reviewing the wine list for us? Do you recommend red or a white? Or maybe a nice rosé?"

"Bite me," she said, heading back to the kitchen.

I watched both men construct wahoo tacos and sat back as they took their first bite. They both purred and nodded then took another large bite.

"You have to try this, Suzy," Gerald said. "You won't believe how good it is."

"No, that's okay," I said, shaking my head. "I'll take your word for it."

"No, I'm serious," Gerald said, holding his taco out for me to sample. "Actually, I'm going to have to insist. Take a bite."

"I know where your fingers have been, Gerald," I said, frowning.

"Then just taste a small piece of the wahoo," he said. "If you don't like it, I'll buy you lunch for the next month."

"Well, since I never turn down free food," I said, reaching for the smallest piece of fish I could find on the tray. I slowly worked it into my mouth and chewed. Then my eyes grew wide. "Oh my God."

"Told ya," Gerald said, getting back to work on his taco.

I quickly built one of my own and took a big bite. I swallowed then exhaled loudly.

"That tartar sauce is incredible," I said.

"It's all incredible," Detective Renfro said, reaching for another flour tortilla. "What did Ramon say about somebody owing him money?"

"He said he'd done a few odd jobs for the company that was about to hire him, but they never paid him," I said, polishing off the first of what I was now sure would be several tacos. "Ramon specifically mentioned import-export so he must have been promised a job by somebody from Jensen's company."

"Well, then it has to be one of the people staying at Jennifer's place, right?" Detective Renfro said.

"Yeah, I agree," I said.

"You think you can come up with a plausible excuse to drop by there again?" the detective said.

"I'm sure I can."

"That's going to be a problem," Gerald said, wiping his mouth. "Jen told me they all flew out yesterday."

"What?" Detective Renfro said, shocked.

"I thought you had some people assigned to keep an eye on them," I said to the detective.

"I do," he said, frowning. "And they're under strict orders to keep me in the loop."

"Unless they were told to drop their surveillance," I said. "Apart from you, who else could do that?"

"The Commissioner," Gerald said, glancing back and forth at us.

"What the heck is going on around here?" Detective Renfro said, getting to his feet. "Excuse me for a moment. I need to make a phone call."

"Most interesting," Gerald said as he meticulously built another taco. "As always, the Commissioner is full of surprises."

"You think he's covering something up?" I said.

"Possibly," Gerald said, taking a bite. "But what's more likely is that the Commissioner is merely trying to put a crimp in Detective Renfro's investigation."

"Just because Renfro's career is taking off?" I said, frowning.

"The Commissioner never likes any of his underlings getting too much publicity. Or getting too comfortable."

"Even though he's trying to solve a high-profile murder case?" I said.

"All the more reason," Gerald said with a shrug. "These tacos are fantastic."

"That's an incredibly petty thing to do," I said.

"Suzy, you should know by now that power and pettiness aren't mutually exclusive," Gerald said, finally slowing down. He set his half-eaten taco down on his plate and folded his hands in front of him. "And if the Commissioner had his wish, Detective Renfro would simply disappear."

I nodded and toyed with my food until my thoughts coalesced. Then I flinched in my chair and scowled.

"Are you okay?" Gerald said, studying my movements closely.

"I'm fine," I said, staring off into the distance. "Wow. Now, there's an idea."

"What?

Before I could respond, the front door opened and Detective Renfro entered, phone in hand. He sat back down and placed the phone on the table next to him.

"I can't believe it," the detective said. "He reassigned my guys and ordered them not to mention it to anybody. Why would he do that?"

"Think about it," Gerald said, glancing over at him.

"Yeah, I've heard about the Commissioner's tendencies," he said. "But this is the first time he's ever done it to me."

"You've never been a threat to him before. Now you know why he's universally detested by all of us who have to deal with him," Gerald said. "Do you know where their flight went?"

"My guys are doing some digging with the airlines," Detective Renfro said. "It shouldn't take long. I can't believe the Commissioner would do something like that."

"That's nothing," Gerald said. "Trust me, he's done much worse."

"What did I miss while I was outside?" he said.

"I believe Suzy was just getting ready to unveil her latest theory," Gerald said, motioning for me to proceed.

"Hold that thought," Detective Renfro said when his phone chirped. "Renfro...I see...Okay, thanks. I'll call you later." He ended the call and glanced back and forth at us. "The Stoner Twins flew out on Air France to Madrid. The other three went out on Singapore Airlines, not surprisingly, to Singapore."

"From there, they could head to dozens of places in Asia," I said.

"Why does that even matter?" Gerald said.

"It probably doesn't," I said, shrugging. "But it is interesting that they're going back to the area where they'd been working."

"Maybe they just like living in Asia," Gerald said. "But I agree that it would be hard to track them down if they wanted to disappear."

"Assuming we had any plausible reason to track them down," Detective Renfro said, then his eyes settled on me. "Okay, what's your new theory?"

"Actually, it's about a disappearing act," I said.

"Like a magic show?" Detective Renfro said, frowning.

"Yeah, sort of," I said. "Have you ever been to one?"

"A magic show?" the detective said. "Yeah, I've seen a couple."

"And even though you're convinced it's not real, you know, everything is just an illusion, you still have a hard time not believing what you see right in front of your eyes," I said.

"Do you have any idea what she's talking about?" Detective Renfro said to Gerald.

"I was hoping you'd be able to explain it to me," Gerald said, laughing.

"I've got a question for you," I said to Detective Renfro.

"Okay," he said, puzzled.

"Does the Commissioner have any other favorite organizations or charities he's involved with?" I said, glancing back and forth at them.

"What?" the detective said with a blank stare.

"Wow," Gerald said, shaking his head. "I wouldn't have gotten that with a million guesses."

"Does he?" I said, leaning forward.

"Yeah, I think he's pretty involved with the public libraries," Detective Renfro said.

"He is indeed," Gerald said, nodding. "Why do you want to know?"

"Because I want to make another donation."

They both stared at me in disbelief. Then we all glanced at the kitchen when the door opened, and Josie appeared carrying another tray She removed the empty taco tray, replaced our used plates with clean ones, then placed the fresh tray in the center of the table. It contained several different variations of grilled chicken and fish on bamboo skewers along with several dipping sauces and a variety of fruits and cheeses.

"Finally. What took you so long?" I said, glancing up at her. "Oh, I know. You must have been busy doing the dishes."

"Knock it off."

"Could I please get a clean knife?" I said, beaming at her.

"I'd be delighted to do that," Josie said, scowling. "Where would you like it? Perhaps somewhere in the neck?"

"And another pitcher of iced tea for the table."

"Yes, your Majesty."

"Oh, dear," I said, staring down. "It appears that my plate has a smudge on it."

"A smudge?" Josie said, glancing at it.

"Yes, it has a smudge."

"Eat around it," Josie said, then turned and muttered to herself all the way back to the kitchen.

"What did she call you?" Gerald said.

"Oh, I'm not comfortable using that sort of language," I said, laughing as I reached for one of the chicken skewers.

Chapter 27

The main branch of the public library system was located in Georgetown, and like most other places on Grand Cayman, it wasn't far from the water. At the moment, I was sitting by myself at the head table in a small multi-purpose room filled with rows of chairs that would seat about a hundred. There were only a handful of people waiting for the presentation to start, and I was pretty sure the room's capacity wouldn't be tested. My stomach rumbled, but before I could focus on possible dinner options my phone chirped, and I checked the number and answered on the second ring.

"Hey, did you hear anything yet?" I said, keeping my voice low more from learned childhood library behavior than any concern about eavesdroppers.

"You're not going to believe it," Detective Renfro said, barely able to contain his excitement.

"They were there," I said, feeling both proud and surprised by the news.

"They certainly were," he said. "And right in plain sight."

"Wow," I said. "Are they on their way back?"

"They are," Detective Renfro said. "Apparently, they left hours ago. But the idiots forgot to let me know. I'm glad I finally got tired of waiting for an update and gave them a call."

"This could change how we handle things tonight," I said, glancing around the room.

"You haven't done the check presentation yet, have you?"

"No, it's going to be a few minutes before we get started."

"I'm on my way," he said. "But just play it like we talked about. I doubt if he'll try anything in the library, but don't do anything crazy. At least, not until I get there."

"Have a little faith, Detective," I said, ending the call.

I sat quietly, my mind racing from what I'd just learned. But before I could begin processing the information, Wendell Anderson, the head librarian, or whatever title the person who ran the place went by, strolled up and sat down next to me.

"The Commissioner just called and is on his way over," he said. "Again, I can't thank you enough. A mobile book van for children who can't make it to one of our branch libraries is a wonderful idea."

"Don't mention it. I'm happy to do it," I said, deflecting.

Actually, it had been Chef Claire's idea. We'd been trying to come up with a good way to use the money I was about to donate when she suggested kids and books. Josie had then floated the idea of a van stocked with children's books, and it just sort of took off from there.

"How long has the Commissioner been working with the library?" I said.

"Quite a while," Wendell said. "He's big on education, especially reading. He never misses an event like this."

"Yes, I have noticed several library stories and photos in the paper," I said.

"The Commissioner is fond of seeing his picture in the paper, isn't he?" he said, laughing. "What's that old saying, any publicity is good publicity?"

"I guess we're gonna find out," I whispered.

"What?"

"Nothing," I said, glancing at the entrance where the Commissioner was coming through the door trailed by an entourage of four uniformed cops. "There he is."

"I'll be right back," Wendell said, heading off to greet him.

They soon returned to the table, and I stood and shook hands with the Commissioner who was studying my expression closely.

"You're full of surprises, Ms. Chandler," he said, gesturing for me to sit back down. He sat down next to me with Jerome on his other side. "What happened?" he said, chuckling. "Were you worried that your original donation wasn't big enough to get you off my radar?"

"Not at all," I said, shaking my head. "I just wanted to do something nice for the kids."

"Of course," he said, staring off into the distance. "I'm glad you were able to fit today's presentation into your schedule. You've obviously been very busy lately. You know, going out on boats, taking in some of the local sights, dodging assault charges."

He gave me his best crocodile smile and maintained eye contact. Despite the tingle from the hairs on the back of my neck, I forced myself to hang tough. I returned the smile and shrugged.

"Well, since Ramon isn't pressing charges, I guess I don't have to worry about that, right?"

"I'm sure I'll think of something," he said. "You know, Ms. Chandler, most of the people who spend winter down here are happy to just kick back and relax. You seem to be the exception."

"Well, my friends are fond of saying that I am *uniquely weird*," I said, shrugging. "I'm sure your impression of me has something to do with that."

Wendell approached the podium that was next to the table. The Commissioner and I both sat back and focused on the head librarian.

"Perhaps we can continue this discussion after the presentation," the Commissioner whispered.

"Why not?" I whispered back. "Since you're the one who seems to be calling all the shots, how can I say no?"

The Commissioner flinched then rotated his head until I heard a soft pop. I glanced down and couldn't miss the fact that he was clenching and unclenching his hands under the table.

"Did I say something to upset you, Commissioner?" I whispered with a grin.

"Don't push it."

We both sat back and listened as Wendell handled introductions, explained what my donation would be used for, then waited until the polite applause from the crowd of about two dozen died down. He spent a few minutes reviewing several other programs and services the library offered, then finished to another round of applause. The three of us posed for pictures holding another large cardboard check, then Wendell wandered off to mingle.

"If you'll excuse me for a moment," the Commissioner said to me. "I need to have a quick word with my staff. I'll be right back."

"Take your time," I said. "I'm going to wander through the stacks. You'll find me in the mystery section."

"I would have thought you'd be more interested in exploring the self-help books," he said, then headed for his entourage. "Perhaps one that focuses on the importance of minding your own business."

"Yeah, I really need to start working on that," I said as I watched him walk away.

I strolled off toward the stacks feeling much less confident than I'd been earlier today chatting with Rooster and Detective Renfro around the pool. At the time, my plan had been to gently poke the bear to see if I could get the Commissioner to tip his hand, but given the news I'd gotten during my recent phone call, the situation had changed. And if Detective Renfro had heard the latest news, I wouldn't be surprised if the Commissioner was also in the loop. I doubted if he would try to harm me in a public place, but I was convinced that, to him, I was an annoying gnat that needed to be swatted. As I slowly made my way down the empty aisles surrounded by high shelves of books on both sides, I was suddenly feeling very isolated and vulnerable.

I stopped in front of one of the stacks overflowing with mysteries and scanned the titles. Noticing several I wasn't familiar with, I made a mental note to fill out an application for a library card before I left.

Then I felt his presence standing directly behind me.

"Do you like to read mysteries, Commissioner?" I said, not even bothering to turn around.

"No, I'm more of a history buff," he said. "You know, biographies, war, colonial insurrections, stuff like that."

I turned around and tried to read his expression, but got nothing. Given his years as a cop, I wasn't surprised.

"I have to say that I'm perplexed, Ms. Chandler."

"Oh, I hate when that happens," I said, leaning against one of the stacks. "What's bothering you, Commissioner?"

"You, of course," he said, shrugging. "Not to mention the ever-present and increasingly annoying, Detective Renfro."

"But he always speaks so highly of you, Commissioner," I deadpanned.

"I really don't like you," he said as a simple statement of fact. "Way too much money with way too much time on your hands."

"Harsh," I said, shrugging.

"Oh, don't worry," he said, laughing. "We'll get to harsh soon enough."

"Can we chat until then?" I said. "I still have some questions I'd love to get answered before you start doing your thing."

The Commissioner glanced around to make sure we were alone then nodded.

"Sure, why not?" he said, rocking back and forth on his heels. "Actually, I wouldn't mind waiting until it gets dark before I drag you out of here. Knock yourself out."

"Let me guess, you've got the folks from your entourage guarding all the exits?" I said.

"I do always like to keep a police presence around to help me deal with public nuisances," he said, beaming at me.

"Sure, sure," I said. "But I doubt if you'll be putting me in a police car. That would raise too many questions when I didn't show up at the station, right?"

"You've already seen the police station," he said. "I thought you might enjoy visiting someplace different."

"If I wanted to see Ramon's place, I would have agreed to go with him the other day."

"Very good," he said, nodding. "Your reputation is well-deserved. Yes, I'm afraid Ramon insisted that I let him drive today."

"How's his head?" I said. "He took a nasty tumble."

"The condition of his head is irrelevant," the Commissioner said.

"Because as soon as he deals with me, you'll be dealing with him, right?"

"I thought we'd just kill two birds with one stone," he said. "Ramon's place is such a tinderbox. It really wouldn't take much for it to go up in flames."

"You're pretty chatty today, Commissioner," I said, staring at him. "One might even say cocky. How can you be sure I don't have people watching out for me?"

"You came alone, and none of your friends have shown up," he said, shrugging. "And I'm afraid Detective Renfro never made it inside the library."

"Are you sure somebody didn't slip in through the back door?"

The Commissioner stared at me, gave it some thought, then laughed.

"Nice try, Ms. Chandler."

"Yeah, that probably wasn't my best effort," I said. "So, what's the deal, Commissioner? Did you set all this up just to protect your job, or are you more interested in maintaining control of the local drug business?"

"I have no idea what you're talking about," he said, shaking his head.

"I was going to say both, but that might have come across as a bit presumptuous."

"Presumptuous," he said, laughing. "Suddenly, you turn modest? I would have thought you'd be calling your instincts prescient."

"No, I'll leave that to the dog," I said, shaking my head.

He gave me a puzzled frown but said nothing.

"I gotta hand it to you," I said. "Having Ramon blow that yacht up then figuring out a way to pin it on William was a stroke of genius."

"Again, I don't have a clue what you're talking about."

"And the cops on the patrol boat who supposedly found the debris you're using to convict William just happen to be members of your *personal staff*, right?"

"You do have quite an imagination."

"So, you're gonna go down swinging, huh?" I said, nodding. "Okay, fair enough. But I do think it's a pity the Premier won't be able to survive a second scandal involving his son."

"Yes, it's quite tragic. William has made some bad choices. And he does seem to be cut from the same cloth as his father," the Commissioner said.

"I've never met the Premier," I said. "But William seems nice enough. And from what I've seen, he has good taste in women."

The Commissioner gave me his best death stare but let my remark pass without comment.

"You think Gerald is going to be easier to deal with than the Premier?"

"I won't have any problem keeping Gerald in line," he said. "I have a thick file on some of his more *creative* activities."

"Good one, Commissioner. Straight out of the J. Edgar school of how to maintain power," I said, then laughed. "I just hope you look better in a dress than he did."

"Nobody manages to keep their job running the FBI for fifty years without knowing a few things about human behavior. Or about their weaknesses," he said. "And like I said, I'm a big fan of historical biographies. As soon as we take care of William and his father is sent packing, I'll start worrying about Gerald."

"You sound confident."

"The evidence against William is airtight."

"It certainly seems to be," I said. "Well played there, Commissioner. But I do have to wonder why you didn't pay Ramon what you owed him. From what I've seen, you don't want him talking. That seems to be a loose end you don't need."

"Not if he goes up in flames tonight with his new girlfriend," he whispered.

"Fair point," I said. "And Ramon doesn't seem to be the sort of person you could trust to keep his mouth shut."

"When he drinks, he tends to babble. And he drinks all the time."

"I noticed," I said. "And he also tends to tell lies. That was the one big mistake he made."

240

"I'm not following you," he said, his eyes narrowed. "What mistake was that?"

"It's not important," I said, shaking my head. "Since Ramon and I will be human candles at some point tonight, it really shouldn't matter." Then I focused on one of the bookshelves nearby. "Unless, of course, some of the people I've shared my side of the story with start talking."

"You're going to have to do better than that, Ms. Chandler," the Commissioner said with a grin. "Ramon doesn't know anything."

"You mean apart from knowing that you and Jensen were working together to take the Premier out by framing his kid."

The Commissioner laughed a long time, and it reverberated through the empty library.

"Aren't you forgetting something?"

"It certainly wouldn't be the first time," I said, shrugging.

"It would be pretty hard for me to work together with somebody who's already dead," he said.

"Yeah, I'm gonna go with impossible," I said, scanning the titles on the shelf I was focused on.

"There you go. Now, is there anything else you'd like to discuss? I wouldn't mind getting out of here. I have a dinner meeting."

"That's not an invitation to join you, right?"

"Sadly, no," he said, giving me a smug look I so wanted to knock off his face.

I grabbed a book from the shelf and flipped through the pages.

"This is one of my favorites," I said. "You ever read Raymond Chandler?"

"No, I can't say that I have," the Commissioner said, checking his watch.

"That's too bad," I said, staring at the book. "I love his stuff. This one is called *The Long Goodbye*. A lot of people don't agree with me, but I think it's one of his best."

"I deal with enough mystery on the job," he said, shrugging. "The last thing I want to do is go home and read about it at night."

"Yeah, I get that. But Chandler's books are much more than just mystery stories. He was really good at exposing society's seedy underbelly. His books also deal with the lengths people are willing to go in order to preserve the illusion of integrity and maintain their reputation. Especially the rich and powerful who love posing as pillars of virtue, yet are inherently corrupt." I stared at him. "But I understand why you wouldn't want to read it. In your case, that would be like preaching to the choir."

I tossed the book to him, and he fumbled it before finally managing to snatch it out of the air.

"You'd like the plot of *The Long Goodbye*," I said, staring directly into his eyes. "It's about a guy who fakes his own death."

The Commissioner's eye grew wide, and he started to take a step toward me. Then stopped himself and took a couple of deep breaths.

"I think it's time we got going."

"Sure, you probably want to meet Jensen's plane at the airport," I said.

"What?"

"Oh, you haven't heard," I said. "I was sure you would have by now. Maybe Detective Renfro's guys are able to keep a secret. Still, I would have thought somebody might have called and given you a heads up."

"What on earth are you talking about?"

"Jack and Jill Jensen were picked up by the authorities at their island in Sri Lanka," I said. "And they're currently on their way back to Grand Cayman. I can't wait to hear what they have to say for themselves."

"You're bluffing."

But since he was reaching for his holster, I quickly decided he wasn't sure. And he wasn't taking any chances. As he fumbled with the snap on his holster, I took off and did my best lumber down the aisle between the two stacks that towered above me. At the end of the row, I made a right, then a quick left, then another right and ducked down behind a collection of spare tables and chairs. I fought to get air into my lungs as quietly as I could and focused on my breathing. I heard soft footsteps slowly making their way toward me, and I hunched down close to the floor on my hands and knees.

"Ms. Chandler?" the Commissioner called out in a sing-song voice. "Oh, Ms. Chandler? Let's say we make this easy on both of us. I have my people guarding all the exits, and there's no way you're going to get-"

Then I heard a loud thump, punctuated with a guttural grunt, followed by the unmistakable thud of a body falling to the floor. I heard muffled voices, then what sounded like something being dragged across the floor. But I decided my curiosity would have to wait. Still hunkered close to the floor on all fours, I grimaced from the onset of a leg cramp and continued to focus on my breathing.

"Suzy?"

I relaxed and exhaled loudly when I heard Rooster's voice.

"Over here."

"Come on out," Rooster said.

"Where are you?"

"It looks like somewhere in the home and garden section," he said. "Just follow my voice."

I climbed to my feet grimacing from the leg cramp as I limped my way back toward the stacks. I found Rooster and Detective Renfro standing over a very groggy Commissioner who was on the floor with his legs splayed and his hands cuffed behind his back.

"What happened to him?" I said.

"I hit him with a coffee table book," Rooster said.

"Are you sure it wasn't the coffee table?" I said, staring at the lump on the back of the Commissioner's head.

Rooster tossed the thick book on the floor, and it landed with a thud.

"I guess those things just aren't for show," he said, laughing.

"You came in through the back door?" I said, glancing back and forth at them.

"We did," Detective Renfro said. "We were hiding out in the children's section."

"Were you able to hear our conversation?"

"Oh, yeah," Detective Renfro said. "Loud and clear."

"Including the part about how he was planning on setting Ramon and me on fire?"

"We heard it all," Rooster said.

"We just took Ramon into custody. The idiot was parked right behind the library. And the Jensens will be landing later tonight," Detective Renfro said. "I'm betting they'll roll over and try to cut a deal."

"I wish them luck with that," I said, frowning. "Conspiracy to commit murder at a minimum, right?"

"Yeah, that would be a good start," Detective Renfro said. "What do you say, Commissioner? Do you think you'll end up in prison down here, or will the Brits want you serving your sentence back in the home country? Personally, I think some of the folks you've put away here would love to have you as a roommate."

"This isn't over, Detective," the Commissioner said.

"Relax, Commissioner," I said. "Just think about all the time you'll have to catch up on your reading."

Chapter 28

On our way into the police station, we passed Officer Jones heading the other way. I beamed at him and chirped a pleasant greeting, but he only managed a cold stare and did his best to hide his still bandaged hand from view. I guess he'll be holding the grudge awhile. I gave him a wave as he headed out the door, but he ignored me and climbed into the passenger seat of a police car and studiously avoided making eye contact with me.

"He's still taking quite a ribbing," Detective Renfro said. "Don't worry, he'll get over it."

"When?" I said, staring at the police car that was making its way up the street.

"Probably after he has another chance to arrest you," he said, laughing. "Or at least give you a couple traffic tickets."

"When can I talk to the Jensens?" I said, following the detective down the hall.

"You can't," Detective Renfro said. "You're lucky I agreed to let you two even tag along."

"Well, excuse me for solving the case," I said, pouting. "At least give me a few minutes with them so I can find out what they want to do with their dog."

"Maybe," Detective Renfro said. "After I'm done with them."

"Whatever you say…Commissioner," I said, grinning at Rooster.

"Shhh," the detective said, glancing around to check if there were other people within earshot. "Don't start with that."

"Yeah, we don't want to jinx it, right?" I said, veering left and playfully bumping up against his shoulder.

"She decides to spend the winter down here, and you make the conscious choice to *follow* her?" Detective Renfro said to Rooster.

"I know," Rooster said. "But she's still a better option than dealing with that weather."

"Remind me never to visit," Detective Renfro said, coming to a stop. "Okay, you two wait out here. If I get a chance, I'll give you a few minutes to talk to them. About the dog. And only about the dog."

"Sure, sure."

Rooster and I sat down and glanced around the empty room. I stretched out and put my feet up on a chair.

"What time is it?" I said, yawning.

"Almost eleven," Rooster said, flipping through a stack of magazines in front of him before selecting one with a picture of a giant marlin on the cover. "Nice fish. We should call Captain Jack and book another trip."

"Sounds great," I said, stifling another yawn. "Just not tomorrow. I plan on sleeping most of the day."

We chatted for a few minutes, then I drifted off and dreamt of a fortunetelling poodle wearing a purple turban and large hoop earrings. The dog shook water all over me and was just about to reveal my fate when I felt something nudge my foot. I opened my eyes and saw Detective Renfro standing in front of me. I sat up and waited for him to speak.

"Okay, I'm going to give you ten minutes," he said. "Try to control yourself."

"You're so good to me," I said, hopping up and giving him a hug. I started toward the door, but stopped and turned back. "Are they talking?"

"Oh, yeah," he said, grinning. "They're very chatty."

"So, you've got everything you need?"

"Pretty much. Between them and Ramon, it's quite a story. In fact, I'm on my way to go another round with the Commissioner," Detective Renfro said, then narrowed his eyes at me. "Ten minutes. Best behavior. Then you two go home. Okay?"

"Geez, have a little faith, Detective," I said, lumbering toward the door.

I stepped into the same room that Josie and I had been in during our brief incarceration. The Jensens were sitting at the table staring off in different directions. They both looked at me with confused expressions then glanced at each other and shrugged.

"Hi," I said. "I'm Suzy Chandler."

"You don't look like a cop," Jill Jensen said.

"Oh, I'm not a cop," I said, sitting down across from them. "I have your dog."

"What?" Jack Jensen said. "How the heck did that happen?"

"Polly jumped off your yacht just before it blew up," I said, glancing back and forth at them to gauge their reaction.

They looked at each other and shook their heads in disbelief.

"How the heck did she manage to get on the boat?" Jack said to his wife.

"I have no idea," she said, shaking her head. "Weren't you supposed to drop her off at Jennifer's place?"

"No," he said, frowning. "You said you were going to do it."

"I did?" Jill said. "When?"

"Obviously during one of the times when you weren't listening to a word I was saying."

"Don't start," she said, glaring at her husband before focusing on me. "She jumped off the boat?"

"Yeah, she did," I said. "She's lucky we were fishing nearby. She swam to our boat. And she's been staying with us since then."

"So, she's okay?" Jill said.

"She's fine. Just a little spooky to be around at times," I said.

"That's our Polly," Jack said, nodding. "She's an amazing dog."

"Why didn't you take her with you to Sri Lanka?" I said.

"We decided it was better if she wasn't with us," he said.

I let his comment roll around for a few moments then nodded.

"Okay, I get it," I said. "It's harder to slip in and out of different countries unnoticed if you're traveling with a standard poodle. That's something people would remember seeing."

"Yeah," Jack said.

"And dropping her off with your daughter would keep Polly safe without jeopardizing your chances of convincing people you were on the boat."

"We'd never do anything to hurt Polly," Jill said. "And our plan was to get her back from Jennifer as soon as we...resurfaced."

"But somebody forgot to drop her off," Jack said, again glaring at his wife.

"I said I didn't remember us talking about it," she snapped. "Let it go."

"A pretty big oversight, wouldn't you say?" I said.

They both fixed their glares on me, and I eventually shrugged.

"Not that it matters much now," I said. "But how do you think she ended up on the boat?"

"I imagine she thought we were going to leave her behind," Jack said. "And she loves being out on the water. I've given up trying to figure out how she manages to do a lot of the things she does."

"What's going to happen to her?" Jill said.

"She can stay with us until we find a good home for her," I said. "That's one thing you don't have to worry about."

"Thank you," she whispered, then shrugged. "Not that Polly is going to need a new home."

"I'm not so sure about that," I said, glancing back and forth at them.

"I'll bet you a thousand bucks she doesn't," Jack said, leaning forward.

"That's okay. I'd hate to take your money. Would you mind if I asked you a few questions?" I said, leaning forward and placing my elbows on the table.

"As long as you don't mind if we choose not to answer them," Jack said.

"Fair enough," I said, nodding. "This whole thing started when you learned that Jennifer was in a relationship with the Premier's son?"

"Actually, we've been talking about it for a long time. The news about Jennifer and William just brought it to a head," he said.

"I'm sorry," I said, frowning. "But that doesn't make a lot of sense to me."

"I really don't care," he said, shrugging it off.

"I imagine you don't," I said. "What on earth happened between you and the Premier?"

"He had me disbarred," Jack said. "And ruined whatever hopes I had for a political career in the process."

"Okay," I said, frowning. "And you didn't think you deserved to be disbarred?"

"Oh, I'm sure I did," he said, shrugging. "But that's not the point. He was supposed to be my best friend."

"He was the best man at our wedding," Jill said. "Can you believe that?"

"Hey, over the past few days, I've been showered with the remains of exploding roosters, broke up an illegal cockfight, then got arrested and bit a cop. I'll believe pretty much anything you tell me."

"You bit a cop?" Jill said. "Good for you."

"It seemed like a good idea at the time," I said, doing my best to sort through the questions rolling around my head. "So, when the Premier used whatever happened between the two of you to jumpstart his political career, you decided at some point to get revenge?"

"We did," Jill said, glancing at her husband. "And when Jen told us she was getting serious with William, that was the last straw."

"So, you decided to blow up your own yacht?"

"Why not? We have insurance," Jack said, shrugging. "You saw the explosion?"

"Oh, yeah. Couldn't miss it," I said, concentrating hard. "But you're not involved in drug smuggling, are you?"

"No," he said. "I detest drugs."

"But you had some planted on the boat," I said. "Since you were framing William, someone with a police record for drug trafficking, you wanted to make it look like he was...what, protecting his territory?"

"Yeah, I imagine it was something like that," Jack said. "You'll have to get the details from the Commissioner."

"He's involved in drug dealing, isn't he?"

"That would be my guess," Jack said with a shrug. "But I really don't know. Like I said, I detest drugs. Talk to the Commissioner."

"I'm sure they're doing just that at the moment," I said. "But the main thing was setting William up. You knew that his father couldn't survive a second scandal involving his son. The cocaine was just an add-on. A motive sweetener, right?"

"Motive sweetener?" Jack said, giving me a small smile. "Good one. I like that."

"Feel free to use it," I said. "And you got to know Ramon through the cockfights."

"I did," he said. "We both share a love of the sport."

"Sport?" I said, scowling at him. "Baseball's a sport. Cockfighting is barbaric."

254

"To each his own, Ms. Chandler," Jack said.

"I agree with you," Jill said. "I think it's despicable."

"Nobody cares what you think, dear," he said.

I waited out their exchanged dirty looks and mumbled curses to each other before continuing.

"The roosters on the boat were for Ramon?"

"They were," Jack said. "As partial payment for his services."

"Okay," I said, confused.

"They were some amazing fighters," he said.

"I'll take your word for it. But Ramon didn't know they were on the boat, did he?"

"I seriously doubt it," Jack said.

"The Commissioner kept that little nugget to himself," I said. "Along with the stack of cash you gave him to give to Ramon."

"You're good," he said, nodding. "When I expressed my concern about using Ramon, the Commissioner told me not to worry about it. Based on what the detective told me earlier about the Commissioner's plans for Ramon, now I understand why he wasn't worried."

"Ramon was just a loose end," I said, flashing back to my conversation in the library. "By the way, how much does it cost to have someone blow up a yacht?"

"A hundred thousand," Jack said with a casual shrug.

"And some roosters," I said.

"Yes," he said, laughing. "And some roosters."

"You knew that Ramon used to work for William and would be able to figure out a way to steal the explosives from his warehouse."

"Only after the Commissioner told me," he said. "Actually, we weren't involved in any of the details."

"Once the Commissioner was onboard, he told you to just leave everything to him, right?"

"He did. And if you can't trust the top cop to pull something like this off, what can you do?" he said, shrugging.

"I told you using him was a dumb idea," Jill said. "I never trusted that guy."

"You can't trust any of them, Snookums. Use them, but never trust them. How many times do I have to tell you?"

"The Commissioner makes sure the explosion and the murders get pinned on William, then he takes Ramon out of the picture," I said, more to myself than them.

"I thought we just covered that ground," Jack said, frowning at me.

"Yeah, sorry about that," I said.

Then a question floated to the surface.

"So, who was on the boat when it blew up?"

"I have no idea," Jack said, shrugging. "Probably just some local deck hands the Commissioner hired."

"Your compassion is truly touching," I said, shaking my head. "The Commissioner gets his picture in the paper as the protector of virtue and defender against corruption, thereby saving his job. And the Premier slinks off in disgrace."

"Great plan, huh?" Jack said, cocking his head at me.

"Elegant. But a bit elaborate, wouldn't you say? It had a lot of moving parts," I said. "And then at some point in the future, when the Commissioner tells you it's safe to come back, you two resurface with some cover story about how you've been traveling and out of the loop. And you just can't believe the tragic events that have transpired."

"That's pretty close," he said, nodding.

"Where were the two of you supposed to be? It's a bit hard to not hear things these days. Especially a story like that."

"An extended wilderness trek through the Amazon," Jack said with a grin.

"Good one," I said, then glanced back and forth at them. "I have to say that you're both being very casual about all of this."

"We'll be fine," Jack said. "Our lawyer will splash a ton of money around, and I'm sure we'll end up getting probation as long as we agree never to set foot back in Cayman again."

"You see, Suzy," Jill said. "While we may have been involved, we weren't part of the actual execution of the plan."

"Exactly," Jack said. "We were vacationing at our place in Sri Lanka at the time."

"I don't know, guys," I said, shaking my head. "It sounds like a distinction without a difference."

"Well, let's just leave that for the lawyers to quibble over," Jack said.

"Speaking of lawyers," Jill said. "What's keeping that charlatan? We should be bonded out by now."

"I was just thinking the same thing," Jack said. "If this nonsense takes much longer, I'm going to die of hunger. I'm starving."

"Me too," Jill said. "But I doubt if we want to run the risk of eating anything here. God knows what sort of stomach bug we'd pick up."

"Hang in there, Snookums," he said, patting her hand. "I'm sure we'll be out of here soon. Tell you what, we'll swing by the Ritz-Carlton on the way home for a bite."

"It's getting late," she said, glancing down at her watch that was probably worth more than my car.

"Don't worry. I'm sure they'll open one of the restaurants for us if we make it worth their while."

"Oh, that sounds wonderful," she said. "Andiamo?"

"No, I'm not in the mood for Italian," he said, frowning. "How about Blue?"

"Ripert's place?" she said. "Sure, I could go for some seafood. I wonder if Eric's in town."

"There's only one way to find out," he said, squeezing her hand.

I stared at them, open-mouthed.

"What is it?" he said.

258

"Raymond Chandler would have loved you two."

"You know," Jack said, nodding his head. "I've often said the same thing."

Epilogue

With great trepidation and my clothing cinched tight, I entered the Government Administration Building and cautiously glanced around before heading to the front desk to check in. The same security guard glanced up from his computer and grinned when he recognized me.

"Welcome back," he said.

"Yeah, it's me," I said with a blank stare.

"I assume you're here to see the Finance Minister," he said with a smug smile.

"Actually, I'm here to see the Premier."

"Oh, you're moving up in the world," he said, biting his lip to keep from laughing.

"Please, don't start," I said. "This is hard enough as it is."

"I'm sure you'll be just fine," he said, winking at me. "You know the way by now, right?"

"I do," I said, heading for the elevators.

"Oh, Ms. Chandler."

I stopped and turned back to him.

"Yes?"

"Try not to wear him out. He has a very full day ahead of him," the guard said, then couldn't contain his laughter any longer.

"Everybody's a comedian," I said, then wheeled around and did my best lumber toward the elevator.

My phone chirped just before I pressed the up button. I answered the call and leaned against the wall outside the elevator.

"Hi, Victor," I said. "How's the weather in Ottawa?"

"It sucks," he said. "I'll spare you the details."

"Okay," I said, laughing. "What's up?"

"We got a deal," he said.

"Really? Wow, you work fast."

"The board was all over it. I got you fifteen million and the hundred thousand shares."

"Well done," I said, feeling the last of the company-induced weight fall off my shoulders. "Now what?"

"I'm going to Fed Ex the documents to you today. Take a look, then sign the contract and get it back to me. Then we'll wire the money to your account."

"Perfect," I said, grinning. "It was nice doing business with you, Victor."

"I still think you're nuts," he said, laughing.

"Think? You have doubts?" I said.

"I'll be talking with you soon," he said. "Try to stay out of trouble."

"I'm afraid it's a little late for that," I said, remembering why I was here.

261

I ended the call and rode the elevator then made my way toward the Premier's office and was greeted by his executive assistant. I stood waiting as she called him on the phone then escorted me inside. He got up from behind his desk when I entered and smiled at me.

"Mr. Chandler," he said, extending his hand. "It's a pleasure to meet you." Then he gestured at a sitting area, and I recoiled when I saw Gerald on a couch next to a woman I didn't recognize.

"Of course, you know Gerald," the Premier said.

"Hey," I said. "How's it going?"

"Hello, Suzy," Gerald said, getting up to give me a hug that helped me relax a bit.

"I'd like you to meet the Governor of the Cayman Islands, Henrietta Williamson," the Premier said.

"It's nice to meet you, Ms. Chandler," she said, also standing to shake my hand.

"The pleasure is all mine," I said, still incredibly nervous about the reason I'd been called to the Premier's office. "But please call me Suzy."

"Suzy it is," she said, smiling.

"So, can I call you Gov?" I said, for reasons unknown. I silently cursed myself and did my best to maintain my composure.

"It's probably better if you don't, the Governor said, giving me a puzzled look. "Henrietta will be just fine."

"Okay," I said, exhaling audibly as I rocked back and forth on my feet. "No cops or lawyers, huh?"

"What?" the Premier said, glancing back and forth at Gerald and the Governor.

"This is some sort of deportation hearing, right?" I said, squeezing my hands to keep them from shaking. "I just assumed there'd be some cops and lawyers hanging around."

"Why on earth would you think you're being deported?" Gerald said, staring at me in disbelief.

"Well, when Detective Renfro told me the Premier wanted to speak with me, he sort of led me to believe that…" I said, then scowled. "I'm gonna kill him."

"I think Detective Renfro was having a little fun with you," the Premier said, laughing. "Actually, I asked you to stop by so I could thank you."

"You did?" I said, staring at him.

"Yes, please have a seat," he said, gesturing at a chair near the couch.

I sat down and got as comfortable as I could manage. I looked around and frowned.

"I'm sorry to do this," I said. "But my knowledge of how your government works is a bit sketchy."

"What do you need to know?" the Premier said.

"You're the Premier, so you run the place, right?"

"Actually, the Governor, as the Queen's representative, technically *runs the place* as you so eloquently put it. She's the de facto head of state. But, yes, I am responsible for the day to day running of the government."

"And you're an elected member of the Legislative Assembly?"

"Yes, Gerald and I both have our own constituents we represent," the Premier said.

"So, you're not actually elected as Premier?" I said.

"No," the Governor said. "I appoint the leader of the ruling party as the Premier. And I serve as Governor at the Queen's pleasure. I have a four-year appointment."

"It sounds complicated," I said with a frown. "But given our elections lately, who am I to be talking about strange politics?"

"Indeed," the Governor said, laughing.

"Please accept my sincerest gratitude for helping William get out from underneath the problem he was dealing with," the Premier said. "I truly can't thank you enough."

"Don't mention it," I said, shrugging it off. "I was sure he was innocent. And then I just sort of got caught up in events as they unfolded."

"Yes, so I hear," the Premier said. "Detective Renfro said he couldn't have done it without your help." Then he caught and held my eyes. "Not that I was thrilled to hear that a part-time resident was involved in an active police investigation."

"Yeah, I really need to start working on that." Then I glanced at the Governor who was studying me closely. "No offense, Governor, but why are you here?"

"I've heard so much about you the past several months from Gerald," she said, smiling. "I just couldn't pass up the chance to finally meet the Naked Lady."

My face flushed deep red with embarrassment, and I glared at Gerald.

"Don't look at me. I didn't tell her," he said, laughing.

"It was your assistant, wasn't it?" I said.

"Maybe."

"Is that all you wanted?" I said, glancing around. "I'm supposed to meet everyone at the docks soon. We're taking the dogs out and maybe do a bit of fishing."

"If you have a few minutes, we do have a bit of news to share with you," the Premier said.

"Is it about the Jensens?"

"Actually, that wasn't what I was referring to, but we do have some news on that front," he said.

"When I spoke to them, they were convinced they were going to get probation," I said.

"That is a distinct possibility," the Governor said. "Along with a permanent ban on living anywhere within her Majesty's Commonwealth."

"Interesting," I said, giving her a small smile. "Trying to keep the riff-raff out, right?"

"Among other things," the Governor said.

"What about the Commissioner?" I said.

"Oh, he's going to prison for a very long time," the Premier said with a huge grin. "Along with several other corrupt cops who did his bidding."

"Good call," I said, nodding. "And Ramon?"

"The same," the Premier said. "And hopefully for just as long."

"So, who's going to be the new Commissioner?" I said, glancing back and forth at the Premier and the Governor. He gestured for her to take the lead.

"Historically, the Police Commissioner has been filled by someone from the UK," the Governor said. "But given recent events, I imagine her Majesty would strongly consider our recommendation that it be filled by someone local."

"You're giving the job to Detective Renfro?" I said to the Premier.

"Well, that will be a decision for the Governor and Gerald to make," he said, letting his comment hang in the air.

I frowned, then the lightbulb flickered and finally held. I shook my head as if to clear the cobwebs.

"Really?"

"Yes," the Premier said. "I've decided to step down. Frankly, I've had enough. Trust me, I'd much rather be spending the rest of the day with you fishing."

"There's plenty of room on the boat," I said, still thoroughly confused.

"Maybe some other time," the Premier said, laughing. "At the moment, I'm rather busy with some transition activities. Not to mention trying to rebuild my relationship with my son and his new fiancé."

"They got engaged?" I said, glancing at Gerald who, judging from his blank expression, had already heard the news.

"They did," he said. "And I'm about to become a grandfather."

"Jennifer's pregnant?" I said, sneaking another look at Gerald.

"She is," the Premier said. "And I couldn't be happier. Maybe I won't make the same mistakes with my grandkids as I did with William. This time I'll do everything I can to be available."

"Good for you," I said, then focused on Gerald. "When do I have to start calling you Premier?"

"You don't," he said. "Gerald will be just fine."

"Sure, sure. Congratulations...Premier."

"Didn't I tell you she was an absolute delight?" Gerald deadpanned to the Governor. "And I think I'd like to take you up on your suggestion that I get a dog. I'm thinking about a poodle. That is if you still have her."

"We do. And there's no way we're going to give her back to those two," I said, firmly. "You're okay with that, right?"

"I'm sure we can negotiate custody of the dog into the agreement," Gerald said. "As you might imagine, the Jensen's leverage is a bit limited these days."

"They should be going to prison," I blurted, then glanced around, chagrined. "Not that it's any of my business. You really want to adopt Polly?"

"If it's okay with you," Gerald said. "If the dog is as smart as you say, maybe she'll be able to give me a hand from time to time. I'm certainly going to need all the help I can get."

"Wow," I said, shaking my head. "You're going to be running the government. Does my mother know yet?"

"No, I thought I'd tell her over dinner tonight," he said. "Try not to let it slip out on the boat today."

"I'll do my best," I said, nodding. "But you're still going to be able to make it to my wedding, right?"

"Of course. I wouldn't miss that for anything. Don't forget to give my assistant a call when you set the date just to make sure it gets on my calendar."

"I'll do that. Just as soon as my mom lets me know," I said with a shrug.

"Your mother is picking your wedding date?" the Governor said with a frown. "You're joking, right?"

Gerald and I grinned at each other then looked at the Governor.

"No," we said in unison.

www.ingramcontent.com/pod-product-compliance
Lightning Source LLC
Chambersburg PA
CBHW070728280626
47159CB00023B/2861